Bad Boys of Hockey

Logan

Jack

Rory

Cooper

Verona

Dean

Austin

Although these novels can be read as standalone stories, reading them in the above order will give you a fuller experience.

4

– 1 –

AUSTIN

Summer in Woodstock, Tennessee is coming to an end and I've got the sunburn to prove it. I always forget how much I love being home until I'm fishin' in the lake, sittin' by the campfire, or goin' to the county fair to eat corn on the cob.

"Summer always goes by way too fast, don't it?"

It's eight in the morning and I'm sitting in the passenger seat of Joe's massive red pickup truck. Country music is playing softly on the radio as my best friend drives us to Applelooza, the summer county fair.

"At least you're here for your birthday this time," Joe says. "I'm fixin' to party my freakin' ass off."

"Hey, look at you sayin' fixin'. You're more of a southern boy than I am!"

He laughs. "I'm gettin' there."

Joe and his family moved to Tennessee when he was thirteen. The Lawless family included his younger sister,

5

Grace, and their mom, Jill. Before that, they lived in New Jersey, California, Arizona, and Texas. Eventually, they made their way here to Woodstock. Their dad was an abusive cheater who Jill left long ago. From long talks with Grace, I found out that they were in and out of shelters a lot but they were strong enough to rise above those circumstances. When they came to Tennessee, they obviously didn't have southern accents, but Joe's been here long enough that he's startin' to get one. His accent ain't as thick as everyone else's, but it's starting to slip out more and more.

"I've been in Tennessee for eleven years," Joe says. "I better have an accent by now."

"Eleven years? Dang. Time sure flies."

"And now that I've opened up Sparkle and Shine, I'm ready to stay here for the long haul."

Sparkle and Shine is his car wash business. He's been wanting to be an entrepreneur since I met him. Halfway through our senior year, his mom died. He finished high school and put his entire inheritance into his business idea—a high-end car wash experience. Extras included rainbow-colored suds and water guns that can be controlled by the customers. Sparkle and Shine ain't all gimmicks though—the technology is incomparable and the high-tech vacuums don't leave a single speck of dust behind.

"I gotta say, Joe. Sparkle and Shine is doin' pretty good. I'm impressed."

"Pretty good? I've got twelve locations across Tennessee! Not too bad, huh? Especially since I've always been a C-student."

I chuckle. "And to think that our high school math teacher—Ms. Matthews—said you'd never amount to anything."

6

Joe grins, showing off the mess of facial hair on his upper lip. It's almost as messy as the hair on his head. "I showed her, didn't I?"

"Sure did."

"We both did. Who woulda thought we'd be this successful? You playin' for a big-league hockey team, and me with my business."

"We can't complain, that's for sure."

He pulls onto the county road toward Applelooza. We approach the large farmer's field transformed into a makeshift parking lot. The orange sun is beaming over the county grounds, lighting up the Ferris wheel, roller coasters, and other carnival rides. Joe pulls into a big empty space near the entrance. His team of Sparkle and Shine employees are already wearing their purple branded t-shirts and are there waiting for him. They've got buckets and sponges in hand.

"Last day for free car washes," he says. "Let's see how much interest we get today!"

"This marketing is genius."

"Ain't it? We've already made a fortune in tips!" Joe pulls the parking brake before rubbing his hands together. "*And* the old ladies love me. There's no way they're not coming to Sparkle and Shine after this."

"I guess you've always had that charismatic rascal vibe that attracts moms and grandmas."

He laughs. "If it works, it works."

"Maybe you'll finally find love."

"Ha! With the state of the dating scene in Tennessee right now? Maybe it's time I date a cougar."

"The datin' scene can't be that bad, can it?"

"You've been here all summer… tell me, how were those few dates with Mary-Beth?"

I chuckle. "Good point."

We climb out of the car. The grass beneath my boots feels slippery with that morning's dew. As I collect my hockey sticks from the back of Joe's giant red truck, I notice his eyes light up.

"Hey! You should hang out with us today," he says. "We'd make even more tips if you join us. People would pay extra to have a hockey player wash their car."

"No, thanks. I promised to have the hockey booth open today."

"Gonna whoop some kids' asses at hockey?"

I smirk. "That's the plan. As long as I ain't givin' anyone a black eye, today's gonna be a good day." I look up at the blue skies and wispy white clouds. "Even the weather's behavin'. Not like yesterday. It was hotter than two squirrels screwin' in a wool sock."

"We were fine out here with the hoses runnin'."

"Yeah, I'm sure you were." I start to pull away.

"Hey! You gonna play hockey in those cowboy boots?" He asks. "And that cowboy hat?"

"You got a problem with it?"

He laughs. "I might come by and film ya later!"

"I dare you to."

"Maybe I'll even try scoring on you!"

I give him the finger.

He laughs. "Oh! By the way, did you make sure you're free tomorrow?"

"Yeah. You asked me this already."

"I'm just double-checking. I'm throwing you the birthday party of the fuckin' century, man. I don't want you accidentally endin' up at some crappy Mexican restaurant with Mary-Beth."

I chuckle. "Don't worry, I'm savin' my last day in Woodstock for you."

"We'll celebrate like old times."

"We might regret that."

Joe smiles deviously. "Naw, never. Promise me you're gonna party with me."

"As long as I don't miss my flight the next day, I'll party as hard as I can."

Lifting his hand, he high-fives me. "Yeah, baby. That's what I'm talkin' about!"

"One condition," I say. "I get to crash in the upstairs bedroom. I don't wanna even *think* about drivin' home."

Joe shakes his head. "No can do, brother. But you can have the basement."

"You savin' the bedroom for someone?"

"Grace is sleeping there."

My gaze snaps in his direction. "Grace? Your sister?"

"That's right."

"She's back?"

Joe nods. "She called me two nights ago crying, asking me to buy her the first ticket out of Thailand."

"Wow." My stomach suddenly feels tight. "That's unexpected."

I haven't seen Joe's little sister in years.

"I'm telling ya, those tickets aren't cheap!" Joe huffs. "Three thousand dollars. Can you believe that? She's lucky to have me."

"Any idea what happened?"

Joe half-shrugs. "She didn't say. She said she had no wallet, no phone—I'm assuming she got robbed."

"Robbed?" Heat floods my body and my muscles tense. "By who?"

9

"I don't know… she mentioned a guy at the hostel. Maybe they were dating or somethin'?"

"Grace datin'?"

Of course, it's been a long time since high school. Grace is not a teenager anymore. My mind races with all the possibilities of what could happen.

He sighs. "Whatever. Haven't seen her in a year and this is how she comes back? She called me at two in the mornin' last night askin' for a ride home from the airport."

"How did she seem?"

"Don't know. I ordered a ride for her on my phone and went back to sleep. Haven't seen her yet. I doubt she'll be too excited. It's not like she wants to be here, anyway."

I stare at the carnival grounds. The Ferris wheel is slowly starting to rotate and wake up for the day. My mind is busy skipping ahead to potential possibilities involving Grace.

"You think she'll be at the party tomorrow?"

Joe is pulling buckets and bags of sponges out of the back of his red truck. "Maybe. Probably. I mean, she'll be at the house."

The Sparkle and Shine employees start calling out for Joe's attention.

"I gotta go," he says. "Maybe we can play some skeeball later or somethin'?"

"Sounds good."

He points at my hockey sticks. "Don't destroy those kids too badly today!"

"Heh. No promises!"

Joe pulls away toward the makeshift car wash area. I pull away in the other direction toward the festival grounds.

Walking with my hockey sticks in hand, I think about Grace Lawless. For years, she was just Joe's little sister—

10

basically my little sister too. She was always around—hanging out with us, having dinner, sittin' on the couch, and watchin' TV. The last time I saw her was the day after her sixteenth birthday. I remember because our birthdays were only two days apart and I was about to turn eighteen the next day. That was the year I moved away to join the hockey development program in Michigan. I remember that night because I was hanging out in their basement one last time. Joe left to get snacks, so I was alone with Grace. She wished me luck and told me she'd miss me… and then she kissed me.

I remember all the emotions like it was yesterday—I was shocked, excited, confused. I never really thought about her in that way until that moment. Why would I? She was Joe's little sister. But when it happened, it suddenly made sense. Lookin' back, my favorite high school memories were the times I spent hangin' out with her on the couch in their basement. She was interestin' and fun to be around.

But I didn't kiss her back. I didn't pull away either. What the hell was I supposed to do? She was my best friend's sister. And I was movin' halfway across the country the next day anyway. Nothin' would have happened between us. It was too little too late.

That night was the last time I saw her. I texted her a few days later but she never responded. I never told Joe or anyone else. Each time I visited Tennessee after that, she was nowhere to be seen. She left Tennessee two years later when she graduated high school. She disappeared like a ghost. There's been no trace of her online—no pictures, nothin'. I only get bits of information about her travels from Joe and Ma's gossipin' girlfriends whenever I'm in town. She's clearly moved on. And based on the way she avoids Tennessee, I'm guessin' she has no desire to relive the past.

But now she's back—whether she wants to be or not. My mind races with potential possibilities. I'm only here for another fifty-two hours before headin' back to Seattle for the new hockey season. I wonder if I'll get a chance to see her or if she's still hidin' from me, ghostin' me. I wonder if she's the same person she's always been or if she's someone new. Either way, I'm lookin' forward to findin' out.

– 2 –

GRACE

Forty hours ago I was in Thailand, and now I'm back in Tennessee. Not by choice. That scumbag American I slept with at the Phuket hostel stole my backpack and everything in it. I woke up two days ago with no phone, no wallet, and no idea what to do. Thank god I had my passport. I got into the habit of hiding it under my pillow after an incident at the Frankfurt airport a few years ago.

After realizing I had been robbed, I tried to find a job. If I could make enough money for some food and a room, I'd be okay. But looking for jobs without a phone was difficult... *really* difficult. And getting a full meal was even harder. I thought maybe some fellow travelers at the hostel could help me out, but the hostel only had a few foreign travelers who didn't understand what I was asking. After a night of sleeping on the streets of Phuket, I woke up realizing I was homeless and broke. It took less than a day for me to tuck my tail between my legs and admit defeat. I called my brother, Joe, for help. After thirty-six hours of

13

traveling through four different airports (on my birthday, no less), I'm finally home.

Home.

It's such a weird word. I haven't lived in Tennessee since I graduated from high school over four years ago. Where is home, anyway? I was born in New Jersey, but I've lived in California, Arizona, Texas, and Tennessee. And over the last four years, I've lived in more countries than I can remember—Chile, Peru, Kenya, Malawi, Thailand, and a few others I'm probably missing. It feels like home is nowhere and everywhere. Joe still lives here, obviously. He's been living in our old house all this time. It's great because I always have a place to come back to. But I can't remember the last time I considered this home. The house—and the city—remind me too much of high school. That was back when Mom was still alive. That life seems so far away now. Tennessee brings back all sorts of memories that I don't need to relive.

I was originally hoping that my first day back would be quiet and low-key. After all, I had no intention of coming back. But once my friend Crystal found out that I was in town, she insisted that we meet up. Today is an especially weird day to be back—it's the last day of Applelooza. I didn't intend on making an appearance but I can't say no to Crystal.

"I can't believe you're back in time for Applelooza," Crystal says. We're sipping on slushy iced coffees as we walk through the grounds of the fair. "I swear I'm happier than a butcher's dog."

"That was really good timing." My iced coffee is starting to sweat in my hand as the afternoon sun moves through the sky. "I don't even know why I'm drinking this… I think I have caffeine from four different airports in my system right now."

14

"What time did you get in last night anyway?"

"Two-ish? I finally got to sleep around four."

"At least you got *some* sleep."

I half-shrug. "Sort of. My internal clock is all off. I think I've only had six hours of sleep in the last three days."

"Well, a county fair is the perfect thing to perk you right up!" Crystal is way too chipper for me right now. A roller coaster rattles by, bringing the sound of screaming teenagers.

"I can't believe I'm here," I say. "Not just at Applelooza... but in Tennessee. I remember coming to Applelooza all the time when I was younger. It's weird being back."

"If only you were here yesterday for your birthday. Hey, let me buy you a birthday present!"

I laugh. "The only thing on my wishlist is a churro with caramel dipping sauce. It's one of the few things I craved when I was overseas."

"Churro with dippin' sauce? Easy peasy. Let's go."

We walk through the chaos of the fair. It's the early afternoon—still bright but the dizzying lights of the rides are starting to flash. Pop music blares through speakers as the scent of hot dogs, apple pie, and fresh-popped buttered popcorn waft through the air. Looking around, I see children, families, teenagers—all sorts of people having fun. A colorful sign is advertising bacon-wrapped chocolate bars while a tent nearby is offering palm readings.

"This isn't what I expected to do my first day back in Tennessee," I say.

"This is the *best* thing to do on your first day back! People are gonna be shocked to see you!"

"That's what I'm afraid of," I mumble.

"You tried bein' sneaky by randomly showin' up without tellin' anyone, but that only gets you so far."

I smirk. "The perks of a small town, huh?"

She laughs. "That's Woodstock for ya. Didn't you miss us?"

"I definitely missed you."

"Oh!" She hugs me. "Please tell me you're stayin'!"

"I don't know… I haven't thought that far ahead." I gnaw at my lower lip. "I guess I'll have to get a job and save up some money."

"Oh, yes! I can help you with that. Preferably somethin' not too busy. We have a lot of hanging out to catch up on!" She puts her arm around my shoulders as we walk. "I'm glad you're back for good."

"Well, I'm not back *for good*."

At least, I don't think so. After the incident with that douchebag in Phuket, I'm not sure I ever want to stay at a hostel again. It's making me rethink wanting to travel at all now. I've always been an independent and carefree woman, but having everything taken from me was a very sobering experience. I know now that I can't be in control all the time.

"Okay, sure," Crystal says. "You're not back *for good*… but this isn't just like a weekend visit like when you came back last Easter. You're actually gonna be here a while."

"Or maybe just three or four weeks."

She stops. "Grace Lawless, why are you making this harder than an advanced calculus exam?"

I exhale heavily. "I just don't want you to get your hopes up. I don't know what I'm doing, so I don't want to make any promises."

"Nuh-uh." She holds tighter onto my arm. "You're not leavin' again, not without me."

16

"Maybe we can travel together."

She curls her lip. "Hmm. Maybe. What's so great about travellin' anyway?"

"It's just so freeing… I feel so independent when I'm out there on my own, you know?"

"I don't have to travel two-thousand miles to be independent," Crystal says. "I get that feeling when I buy myself fancy hair oils."

I laugh. "Yeah, but don't you want to see new places? New oceans?"

"Sure…"

"And volunteering is so fulfilling."

"I'm not traveling halfway around the world to do volunteer work," she says. "If I travel that far, I want an all-inclusive resort, air conditioning, classy restaurants, massages…"

"I can guarantee that you won't like staying at a hostel then."

"Is that one of those places where you gotta share a room with a stranger? Ha! No, thank you." She pauses. "Hold on. Isn't that where you were robbed?"

"Wait… what? How do you know that?"

"Joe told me."

"What? When? How has he already told you?"

"He's giving out car washes by the parking lot. You didn't see him on your way in?"

"No… what did he say about me?"

"Well, let me think." Crystal sips on her iced coffee as she thinks. "He said something about your boyfriend robbing you?"

"Ugh." I rub my face.

17

"Is that true? You have a boyfriend? And he robbed you?"

"He wasn't my boyfriend. At least he's not anymore… I don't know what we were. We met on the train and I thought maybe there was something between us. He convinced me that we should travel to Phuket together, so we did. We stayed in a hostel that night and the next morning he was gone with all my stuff."

"Oh, honey. Are you okay?"

I shake my head. "Yeah, I'm just annoyed. I've met a lot of guys over the last four years, and I've been careful not to get too involved, you know? I tell them the same thing every time—we're just having fun, nothing serious. It's hard having a relationship when you're traveling every few months anyway. But I thought this guy was different. I finally put my trust in someone and he completely fucked me over."

"Oh, hon. That sucks," she says. "That sucks harder than a toilet in an airplane bathroom."

"Heh, yeah…"

"I hope you don't let one scumbag turn you off romance."

"Meh… I was already keeping men at an arm's length. They're not getting anywhere near me now."

She leans in. "No more sex?"

"Well, I never said that! I don't need to date someone to have fun."

"Amen, sister."

We continue walking through the festival grounds.

"Come on. I think the churros are that way." Crystal leads the way as we take a right at the Hall of Mirrors. After getting some churros, we eat while we walk. "How about next time, you travel somewhere within the United States? That way, maybe I'll join you."

18

"What's the point of leaving home if you're not going to go as far as possible?"

"At least if you stay in the US, you'd get to be close to me." She smiles and bats her eyelashes. "And Joe, of course."

I smile. "That's true."

"Crystal!" A man with shaggy hair rushes over to us.

"Oh, hey Brad." Crystal smiles sweetly at him. "This is my friend Grace."

I wave at him. He waves back before quickly looking back at Crystal.

"You going to the rodeo later?" He asks.

"Sure, if you'll be there." Her smile looks like a million dollars. Guys have always flocked to her beauty and charisma.

They flirt some more as I awkwardly try to ignore them. Ripping apart the sugary churro, I look at the festival's flashing lights and the gray clouds rolling in overhead. The excess of the fair is more than I'm used to. After living overseas, I'm not used to the visual and auditory chaos that is an American county fair. And not just any fair—this is Applelooza. The colors and noise overload my senses. Obnoxious pop music accompanies the shrieks and screams of children as they drop down the hill of a roller coaster. Meanwhile, I can smell a mix of fried onions, farm animals, and hay. Licking the cinnamon and sugar off my lips, I take a sip of iced coffee to wash it all down. My sticky fingers cling to my cup as I look back at Crystal.

"Okay, see you later," she says. Brad happily walks away before she looks at me. "That guy won't stop talking to me!"

I laugh. "Maybe it's because you keep flirting with him."

"Me? Flirting?"

I raise my eyebrow.

19

"Okay, fine," she says with a coy smile. "I might have flirted a little. He's cute though… right?"

Sipping on my iced coffee, I give her a subtle shrug. "He seems interested in you. That's all that matters, right?"

Crystal waves her hand. "Whatever. I don't have time to hang out with Brad at the rodeo when I could be spending all my time with you."

She grabs my arm again as we walk.

"We have *so* much hanging out to catch up on," she says. "Where do you want to go first?"

I look around. "I don't know. There's so much going on that it's all so overwhelming."

"Okay, well… do you want to feed the butterflies? Or would you rather watch the robot fighting competition?"

"Is the pie-making competition on soon? Do they still sell slices after the competition is over?"

"Ooh, yeah! They do! That's a good idea. And even better because we can pass by the hockey booth and say hi to Austin."

I stop in my tracks. "Austin?"

"Yeah. Austin Berr… you remember him, right? Of course, you do. He's Joe's best friend!"

Of course, I know Austin. We used to spend time together back when we were teenagers. He used to hang out with Joe in our basement whenever Austin didn't have hockey practice. Over the years, Joe's flakiness meant that I was alone with Austin a lot. He wasn't just a dumb jock. He was a lot smarter than he let on. We would talk about philosophy and the universe. Like most people in this town, he was devoutly religious and went to church every Sunday. Meanwhile, I was never shy to tell that I was a proud atheist. Even to this day, I've never touched a bible. I used to stir the pot by grilling him about god and the bible. I did it just

20

to mess with him, but he was unexpectedly open-minded. My obnoxious questions often led to surprisingly deep conversations that kept me up past my bedtime. Chatting with him was effortless. I tried to distance myself from him when he started getting serious about his high school girlfriend. But after my mom died, Austin was there for me. He was my knight in shining armor.

"I thought he'd be back in Seattle," I say. "It's already September. Doesn't the team start training by now?"

If I knew Austin would be here, I would have endured being homeless in Thailand for an extra week if I needed to.

"Maybe he's sticking around for his birthday tomorrow," Crystal says.

Right. His birthday. It's two days after mine. Even though there was a two-year age gap between us, there were always two days of overlap that gave the illusion that we were only a year apart. Two years seemed like an ocean of time back when I was a fifteen-year-old with a crush. Austin was always older and more mature. But now that I'm twenty-two, two years seem like nothing at all.

"There's the booth," Crystal says, pointing at a hockey-themed booth about fifteen feet away. There's a hockey stick and a sign that says *Outshoot a Professional Hockey Player.* I see a tall burly man in a black Blades t-shirt and blue gym shorts. I recognize those blond curls anywhere.

I pause. It's been so long since I've seen Austin—exactly six years. I remember that moment clearly. I was about to start grade eleven and he was a high school graduate. We were sitting on the couch in the basement—our usual spot. It was the night before he was leaving Tennessee. He got accepted into the hockey development program and would be leaving for Michigan the next morning. He was so cute back then with his blond curls and blue eyes. I couldn't let

21

him leave Tennessee without seeing if he felt the way I felt. When the moment was right, I told him that I'd miss him, and when he said he'd miss me too, I leaned in and kissed him. I didn't plan on doing it, but he just looked so perfect that night and I didn't want to regret not trying. But he never kissed me back. I remember looking at him afterward, waiting for him to say something. But all he did was stare at me. It felt like an eternity... second after painful second ticked by as I waited for him to respond. He never did. The only thing that happened was Joe coming down the basement stairs and interrupting us. I couldn't get out of there fast enough.

Ugh. I get a full-body cringe just thinking about it. It was so embarrassing that I didn't even tell Crystal about it. The only person who knows about that moment is Austin. He texted me a few days later about making sure we were "okay" but I couldn't bring myself to respond. What was the point? It was a crush I never should have had, and I *definitely* never should have acted on. I wish I had a machine that could erase it from my memory—and his too. I wonder if he even still remembers that.

Of course he does, my subconscious hisses at me. How can a guy forget about his best friend's little sister kissing him? There's that full-body cringe again. Is there a hypnotist at this fair? Maybe they can hypnotize me into believing it never happened.

"You okay?" Crystal asks. "You're jumpier than a long-tailed cat in a room full of rocking chairs."

I swallow. "I—yeah, of course."

I try to compose myself but it's hard when Austin Berr is standing fifteen feet away. I wish I could just avoid him for the rest of my life. Crystal follows my gaze.

"Wait… do you still have a crush on him?" Her eyes widen.

"Shh." I look around, making sure nobody can hear her. "No, of course not."

"Are you sure? Because you're blushing."

I touch my warm cheeks. "No, I'm not."

She laughs. "If you don't have a crush on him anymore, then you shouldn't have any problem going over and saying hi, right?"

I don't respond.

"Come on," she says, calling my bluff. "Let's go over."

Before I have a chance to resist, she pulls me in Austin's direction.

There goes my plan to avoid him.

— 3 —

GRACE

Crossing my arms, I follow Crystal as we walk over to the hockey-themed booth. Several people have already gathered around and are watching as Austin faces off against a pre-teen boy. Austin defends the net as the boy pushes the puck back and forth, getting ready to take his shot. I watched enough games in high school to know that Austin's not a goalie, but he still has the size and the professional stick-handling skills to defend a net. As the boy takes his shot, Austin easily pokes the puck away.

"Take a second chance," Austin says. His familiar voice is different—it's deeper and more masculine than I remember.

Austin Berr has always been large and intimidating—he was the big burly jock in high school. But he's even bigger and more intimidating now that he's an adult. He was only seventeen the last time I saw him. He clearly had a lot more room to grow. And even though I've seen him on TV, seeing him in person has me mesmerized. His muscles are bigger,

24

his skin more scarred, and he's even got a beard. An aura of danger surrounds him. The man looks so good he's an actual moving violation. I catch myself watching as he defends the net from another shot attempt.

"Last try," he says.

As the boy prepares his last shot, Austin looks over the small crowd. His gaze lands on Crystal before flashing to me. He looks back at the boy before doing a double-take and looking at me again. His wide eyes linger on me for slightly too long. I look down. The boy's stick clacks against the ground. I look up to see Austin pulling his gaze from me and refocusing his attention a half-second too late. The boy shoots and scores.

"*Yes!*" The boy drops the stick with a clang and starts celebrating.

"Good job, little man." Austin shakes the kid's hand. Meanwhile, his blue eyes flash back up to me.

Sucking in a quick breath, I turn to Crystal. "Should we go now?"

"Look, everyone's leavin'! He'll have time to chat."

I groan as I look around at the small crowd starting to disperse. Austin is taking a selfie with the boy. I look around, wondering if there's something or someone who can save me from this moment. Or I could just run and save myself from certain embarrassment. It's too late. Austin is walking over and his eyes are on me. I rub my temple as if I'm warding off a headache that I know I'm about to have.

"Hey!" Crystal says as he approaches. "How's it going, superstar?"

"Doin' alright. You two enjoyin' the fair?"

"Sure are!"

He won't stop staring at me. I try looking away to avoid his gaze but it doesn't work. His eyes still find me. My throat feels tight as I wonder if he'll bring up the kiss.

"Graceless," he finally says. "You're back."

That's the cutesy nickname he gave me all those years ago. He'd call me Graceless because I was so distracted when he was around. The fact that he's using that nickname tells me that I'll never be anything more than his best friend's silly little sister. Still, hearing that name in his velvety Tennessee accent brings back memories I didn't know I had.

"Yeah... aren't you supposed to be back in Seattle?"

He raises his brows. "You upset I'm here?"

"No." It's the most unconvincing 'no' of all time.

He smirks. "I'm just kiddin'... Coach made some last-minute changes to the trainin' schedule this year. Gave me a few extra days to enjoy the festival."

"Oh."

"It's been a long time," he says.

"Yeah..." I spot the net behind him. "It looks like all those early morning practices paid off."

"All that effort and here I am—a professional Applelooza carnival game. Who woulda thought?"

I smirk. He's just as goofy as he used to be.

There's an awkward silence. I speak before he gets a chance to ask me anything. "What's it like finally being a professional hockey player?"

"Well..." He rubs his blond curls. "Aside from the broken bones, missing teeth, and scars, it's great."

He smiles, showing off two missing teeth. There's something weirdly endearing about it.

I can't help but smile back. "It gives you character."

26

His gaze lingers and I get lost in his blue eyes for a bit too long.

"Hey!" Crystal furrows her brow. "You had teeth when I saw you a few days ago at the pizza place!"

"I've got fake ones," he says. "Not all ladies like a guy who's missin' teeth."

There's a sudden burning sensation in my chest.

"I didn't think you'd be the kind of guy who cares about vanity," I say.

He chuckles. "It's Ma. She doesn't like the thought of me getting into fights. I try not to flaunt my injuries in front of her."

The burning sensation disappears.

"That's Austin," Crystal says. "Always a mama's boy."

It's true. No matter how busy he was in high school, he always had time to drive his mom to church. I always found that incredibly sweet.

"Besides," Crystal adds, "you wanna find yourself a girl who'll like you with no teeth at all!"

He chuckles. "Hopefully I don't lose that many."

I laugh as I think about it—Austin with no teeth. As absurd as that image might be, I can still imagine him with that cute goofy smile. As I look around, I catch Austin watching me with a wistful expression in his gaze. I clear my throat and change the subject.

"Joe told me that you bought your mom a new car."

"Yeah, a few years back. It took a while for my parents to accept money from me, but I found that if I just buy them stuff, they'll accept it. I got them a few renovations, some new farmin' equipment, a new car. My whole paycheck goes to them."

"Do you ever spend any of it on yourself?"

Austin's always been a simple man. Besides a nice truck and extra flannel shirts, I'm not sure what else he'd buy for himself.

"I bought a condo last year," he says. "By the water in Seattle."

"Weird…"

"What's weird?"

"Well, you always said you wanted a house with a backyard and a fence, and a wife and kids. The thought of you in a condo is… weird."

"You remember that?"

"Yeah, of course. You used to talk about it *all* the time. I thought you'd have all that by now."

He watches me for a moment. There's a sparkle in his blue eyes. "I'm workin' on it."

I'm mesmerized by him. When he looks at me, I want to look back. When he smiles, I want to smile back.

"What are you two up to, anyway?" He lifts his hockey stick behind his head and places it across the top of his shoulders. As he holds it in place, he gives me a perfect view of his sunkissed biceps and the veins in his forearms.

"Just hangin' out," Crystal says, resting her head on my shoulder. "Catching up on time with Gracie."

"You back for good, Graceless?" His blue eyes watch me carefully.

"Only until I make enough money to leave again."

Crystal sighs in frustration. "The fact that you just got here and already wanna leave hurts worse than a sandpaper slip-and-slide!"

"Hey, I'm not the only person who left," I say. "Austin left first."

"Yeah, but I don't care about Austin."

"Ouch." Austin chuckles and shakes his head. "Dang, Crystal. I thought we were friends."

"Yeah, but Grace is my bestie and she's been gone too long." She hooks her arm in mine as she's been doing all day. "She doesn't even have her Tennessee accent anymore!"

"I noticed that too." Austin's curious blue-eyed gaze continues to linger.

I shake my head. "Did I ever have one?"

"A little bit," he says. "It slipped out every once in a while."

There's a slight smirk on his lips. I have a list of Austin Berr smiles that I love, and this one tops the list. My breath slows as old memories take over.

"So…" I clear my throat. "You'll be sticking around Woodstock for a while?"

I don't know what answer I want to hear. I suspect I'll be disappointed either way.

"Only until the day after tomorrow," he says. "Joe's throwing me a big party for my birthday tomorrow."

"Really?" Crystal's eyes light up.

"Yeah… I'm surprised he didn't tell you."

"Awesome!" Crystal claps in excitement once again. "Can we come?"

I nudge her in the ribs. *"Crystal."*

"It's at your house, so… I think you'll be there no matter what," he says.

Austin's party is going to be at *my* house? Dammit. It'll even harder to avoid him now.

"Happy birthday, by the way," Austin says. "It was yesterday, wasn't it?"

I look up at him with wide eyes. "Yeah… thanks."

"Do anythin' special?"

"Well… I spent seventeen hours on a flight from Qatar to Dallas, and now I'm at Appleooza. So, I guess this is it."

"That's it? At least have some cake or somethin'!"

I smile at how much he seems to care. That's the Austin I remember.

"I bought her a churro," Crystal says. "But don't worry, I'll make the rest of this day special for her!"

"A good night's sleep would be nice." If I just keep deflecting to my jet lag, then maybe we can ignore the big dancing elephant in the room. But Austin is still watching me with a searing gaze. I don't know if the elephant can be ignored any time soon.

"I hope you're stayin' safe, Graceless," Austin says.

Why would he say that?

"I am," I say.

He's infantilizing me again. First with the cutesy nickname and now with this protective macho front that he puts on. Even in high school, he was obsessed with keeping me safe. None of the boys at school were ever good enough for me so he'd scare them off. He always saw me as a little sister that needed protection. And that's how he sees me now. That kiss between us changed nothing.

"Hey, fools!" My brother, Joe, walks up to us, throwing one arm around my shoulder and the other around Crystal's.

"Why do you smell like soap?" I ask, pushing his arm off me.

"My crew is washing cars down by the parking lot. Free advertising for Sparkle and Shine. What are you guys up to?"

Crystal shrugs. "Visiting food stands and tryin' to use the last of our ride tickets. We might go to the rodeo in a bit."

"You wanna go on some rides together?" Joe asks.

30

Crystal looks at me and shrugs. "Sure, but three is an odd number for riding rides."

"Austin can join us," Joe says. "Nobody's in line anyway."

We all look at Austin. He's still balancing the stick over the back of his shoulders. He looks at me as if seeking my approval. I look down, pretending to be interested in my nails.

"Fine," he says. "Just let me lock away the safe and the sticks."

Pulling away, he disappears into a small tent behind the goalie's net. Hoping to come up with a reason not to join them, I look over at Crystal and Joe. They're too busy talking about the new rainbow-colored foam at Sparkle and Shine. They don't know about my kiss with Austin all those years ago. Unless Austin told Joe, which I doubt… I feel another full-body cringe just thinking about it. Austin returns. He's now wearing jeans and cowboy boots. God, he looks good. I touch my cheeks, making sure I'm not bright red from having to live through this.

"Let's go," he says.

As he walks by me, I catch a scent of leather and cedarwood. It smells like cowboy heaven. I have to stop myself from inhaling too deeply as he walks past. Joe and Austin start walking and Crystal follows. Having no choice, I exhale and join her. When the guys pull ahead, I look over at Crystal.

"Do you really want to go to that party?" I ask.

"Sure, why not?"

"I don't know… it might get crazy. You know how those guys are."

"Honey, there's no way we're not goin' to that party. Your brother is the king of this region. Do you know what kind of people will be there?"

31

I sigh. "Whatever."

She narrows her gaze. "It's because of your little crush, isn't it?"

"Crystal, *shh.*" I look at the guys who are a few feet ahead. Luckily, the surrounding music and screams from the rides are so loud that they can't hear us. I lower my voice anyway. "There's no crush. I haven't seen him in six years!"

"I find that doubtful… you're blushin' like a boy scout in a brothel."

"Am I?" I touch my cheeks.

"You can't hide your feelings from me, Gracie. Eventually, the truth will come out harder than a gay guy in college."

I furrow my brow. "How can there be feelings between us when he's leaving in two days?"

"Honey, two days is a lifetime out here in Woodstock."

Looking ahead, I watch Austin's back muscles move as he walks. If two days can be a lifetime, then six years must be an eternity. There's no way we could click like we used to. Conversation used to flow so easily between us—we were curious teenagers having open-minded conversations about anything and everything. And because it was Austin, there was a healthy dose of goofiness thrown in. The colors and sounds of Appleeooza fade away as I get lost in the nostalgia of those memories.

"Hey, guys!" Crystal's voice brings me back to the present. "Haunted house?"

Grabbing the attention of the guys, she points at a haunted rollercoaster nearby.

"Could be fun," Joe says.

"There's nobody in line. Come on!" She leads the way as we follow, making our way to the front of the line. An empty cart rolls into place. All four of us step forward but the teenage attendant stops us.

"Only two to a cart," he says. Sure enough, the carts are only made for two. Knowing I'll sit with Crystal, I look at her to confirm that we'll go first. To my surprise, she pushes Joe forward.

"Joe and I will go together," she says.

Joe shrugs. "Sounds good to me."

He hops into the cart and Crystal gets in after him. Crossing my arms and tapping my foot, I stare at Crystal. She can barely contain her smile. I subtly shake my head at her. She knows *exactly* what she's doing.

"Have fun!" She simply smiles and waves at us as their cart jerks forward.

Austin stands behind me, towering over me as we awkwardly wait for the next cart. I look up and give him a tight smile before looking back at the haunted house.

Austin turns to me. I try to avoid his gaze but it's no use.

"So, you've been travelin' a lot?" He asks.

"That's right."

"Workin'?"

"Volunteering mostly. But I make money with odd jobs—tutoring, babysitting. Hostels aren't very expensive."

"So, why are you back?" He asks bluntly.

"I... umm..." I clear my throat. "No specific reason."

"You sure? Because I don't know anyone who would spend all day on a plane on their birthday." His blue eyes are inescapable.

I shrug a shoulder. "Maybe I just wanted to come back."

"Sounds like you ran into trouble." He lowers his voice. "Are you okay, Graceless? What happened out there?"

Post-traumatic stress vibrates in my mind like a gong as I remember the ordeal I had to go through. I zone out as I remember the shock of being robbed, the rejection at the hostel, and the long night sleeping outside the train station in Phuket. Too much time is ticking by. I need to say something soon before I seem too suspicious.

"I'm okay now," I say.

He puffs out his chest. "Just tell me his name. I'll make him regret ever hurting you."

I laugh but quickly realize he's not joking. "Austin—you don't have to do that."

"I'm serious," he says. "I can tell something horrible happened. I can see it in your eyes. I won't ever let that happen to you again."

The feminist in me is ashamed that it feels this good having Austin "The Bear" Berr protecting me. But I'm determined not to let the incident at the hostel shake me.

Rolling my eyes, I look away and pretend to be bored. "You don't have to protect me. I'm a grown woman, I can take care of myself."

The muscle in Austin's jaw pulses. "I just want to know that you're okay out there, Graceless."

I exhale sharply. "The childish nickname, the overprotective attitude—you're still treating me like a fifteen-year-old girl."

His chest rises and falls. "I don't mean to treat you like that. But I'll always be protective of my friends and family. I'm a protector, a provider. It's who I am."

I exhale slowly. "I'm fine."

An empty cart slides into place. I look up at Austin. He gestures at me to go first. Climbing into the cart, I take my seat as he climbs in next to me. Since he's a large man—a professional hockey player, no less—he takes up more room

34

than he should in the tiny cart. My arm and leg are pressed against his. I can feel just how hot his body is next to mine. The cart lurches forward down a dark tunnel. With my sight obstructed, all I can smell is Austin's masculine scent. Sandalwood and leather—he smells like cowboy heaven. And though I can't see him, I can feel the tension bubbling between us. The walls glow red as an animatronic devil welcomes us into a dark tunnel.

"Looks like we're in hell," Austin says.

"It seems so," I mumble.

I try not to rub against him but it's impossible in this tiny cart. The red light fades to darkness as we go through the dark tunnel.

"Are you still an atheist?" He asks.

The bluntness of the question makes me blurt out laughing. "Where did *that* come from?"

"I'm just wonderin' if hell is scary to you. Back in high school, you always talked about bein' an atheist. If you don't think hell is real, it can't be that scary." His deep voice is weirdly distracting when it's all I can hear in the darkness.

"Hell still exists to me... it just exists in a different form. Loneliness, isolation, depression... that's hell to me."

And so is this.

"And if you must know," I continue, "I'm agnostic now."

"Agnost—what? What in the hell is that?"

I smirk to myself in the dark. "It means I don't have enough knowledge to make any concrete decisions. So, I don't believe... but I don't *not* believe either."

As the light flashes on in the tunnel, I can see him furrow his brow. "But you don't not *not* believe... right?"

"Yeah... I think." I laugh. "I may not worship a god but I bow to serendipity."

He smirks. "Well, it's good to know that you can change your mind."

I spot the small gold cross hanging from his neck. "And you haven't?"

He half-shrugs. "I don't need knowledge to believe. That's why it's called faith."

"That's… a really good point."

There's the witty guy I remember from high school. Even though he pisses me off, he's still just as charismatic now as he was when he was younger. Although I'm trying to keep my eyes to myself, my gaze is drawn to his full lips, and his irresistible blue eyes. Afraid I might do something stupid if I stare too long, I look away.

As the small rollercoaster starts to pick up speed, it jerks left and right through a graveyard before picking up speed and racing toward a brick wall. Just as we're about to hit the brick wall, a zombie pops up and screams. I shriek and instinctively grab Austin's chest. He puts his arms around me. I feel the cart pivot in a different direction.

"It's okay," he says.

I look up into his blue eyes. My instinct is to pull back, but I don't. The way he's holding me feels more intimate than innocent. Or maybe he still thinks of me as that little girl who needs protecting. Either way, this is dangerous. There's no limit to the number of embarrassing things I can do around Austin, and melting into his arms is one of them. I pull back. The sound of thunder and crows plays over the speakers. The fake lightning flashes, throwing us into light and darkness, casting shadows over Austin's face. He's looking at me and only me. I look at his lips… his beautiful pillowy lips. The moment feels *just* perfect for a kiss. I'm leaning in before I even know what I'm doing. My lips press against his. They're just as impossibly soft as they were the

36

first time I kissed him. The sound of another zombie causes me to jump further into his arms. He holds me tighter against him. But he's not kissing me back. Pulling back, I look into his eyes. Red light floods the room, blotting out all the shadows.

"Grace," he says. It's the first time he's said my name—my *actual* name—all day. The way he says it sounds delicious on his lips.

"Yeah?"

His hands are still on my waist, holding me against him. They feel strong, secure. I wait for him to do something—to kiss me, to profess his love for me, *anything*. But he doesn't do either of those things. The oppressive red light prevents me from reading his expression. My stomach sinks as I realize I'm experiencing a horrible sense of deja-vu.

Great. Another embarrassing moment to cringe about for the next six years.

Our cart goes down a small dip before emerging into the sunshine right where we started. Austin blinks into the sunlight as he pulls his gaze away from me.

"Guys!" Joe calls out.

Crystal and Joe are standing at the exit waiting for us. Austin pulls his hands off me. His eyes linger for a moment. He's unreadable. Those blue eyes are watching me—for what? To see if I'll be heartbroken? To see if I'll beg him to kiss me back? All I want is to get as far away from Applelooza and Austin Berr as possible.

Climbing out of the cart, I make my way over to Crystal.

"Was it scary?" She asks.

"A nightmare." I cross my arms as I look back.

Austin is acting as if nothing happened as he rejoins Joe. My vision grows blurry and I feel a sharp pain in my chest. He was flirting with me a minute ago, and now his brooding gaze is staring off in every direction but me. As I fend off tears, I think about ways to escape. Maybe I can go on a road trip tomorrow and miss Austin's party. If he's so annoyed with me kissing him, then I'll do him a favor and never see him again—just like I tried to do last time. And if Crystal tries to drag me to the party, I won't make it easy for her. I just have to live through two more days and Austin will be gone. And once he's gone, I can figure out what the hell I'm doing in Tennessee. Maybe I'll move to Botswana or Chile… or maybe I'll move as far away from Austin Berr as I can possibly get. The furthest place from Seattle is Madagascar. Maybe I'll go there.

"Let's keep going!" Joe says. Austin joins him as they continue ahead.

And just like that, I know what it's like to be rejected by Austin Berr. *Twice.*

— 4 —

AUSTIN

What the hell is happening?

I feel like I just saw a ghost—and not the kind from the haunted house. After six years, I was starting to believe that Grace was just a figment of my imagination. But now she's here and she's *definitely* not a ghost. She's as real as the scars on my knuckles.

Looking back behind me, I catch her gaze. She looks like a whole new person. The tan and freckles across her nose make me think she's been living in a tent on the beach somewhere. Even her usual raven hair shines auburn in the sun. I barely recognized her until I saw those hazel eyes. They're the same hazel eyes I used to gaze into during those late-night talks on Joe's basement couch. It feels like a whole lifetime has gone by since then. She's a young woman now. Young, but not naive. She's never been naive. She was always the most mature girl I knew in high school. The most beautiful too.

And her lips—they're just the way I remember 'em. The way she wrapped her hand around the back of my head and guided my lips to hers. No waitin' or hesitatin'. She just goes for what she wants. She always has.

Pulling my gaze away, I try to avoid hers. It feels wrong. Joe is the most important person to me besides my Ma. I can't disrespect my best buddy like that. *But* I didn't expect things with Grace to pick up the way they did. Conversation between us flows just as easily as it did six years ago. I forgot what it was like to have a connection like that with a woman.

A woman.

It's weird thinking of her like that. Graceless is all grown up.

"—exactly what I said. You know what I mean?" Joe asks.

"Huh?" I look at him, realizing that he's been droning on for a few minutes now. I guess that means he doesn't suspect anything. He's never been very aware. "Oh yeah, interesting."

"No, it's *not* interesting," he says. "It's annoying. Are you even paying attention?"

I sigh. "There's too much goin' on right now."

It ain't a lie.

"That haunted house must've really gotten to you," he says. "I knew you were a scaredy-cat, but come on, man!"

"Heh, yeah. Never been afraid of ghosts before." I clear my throat before looking back at Grace.

The way she keeps looking down makes her look like a sad angel. She's feminine in a way that I ain't used to. She's strong and independent—that's true, but I see softness and vulnerability too. As her gaze flashes up to me, I see a wistful sadness in her eyes. What the hell happened to her out in Thailand?

40

"Where should we go next?" Joe asks. "We've got twenty minutes before the pie-making competition starts."

"Let's head in that direction," Crystal says. "We can stop at the Ferris wheel on our way… I think we can all get on the same cart!"

"Weren't we supposed to go to the rodeo?" Grace asks.

"But the pie-making competition," Joe says. "It's the best part of the fair!"

"We can't." Grace pulls at Crystal's arm. "We already promised we'd meet someone."

"Well, we don't *have* to go," Crystal says.

"Yes, we do," Grace insists. "We promised Brad, remember?"

Brad? A surge of heat rushes through my veins. I've always been protective when it comes to Grace. It's an old instinct that's hard to stamp out. Protecting my people is what I do. I do it for the guys on the Blades, I do it for my family, and I do it for Grace. The guys back in high school never had a chance with her. I made sure they knew they'd have to deal with me if they ever broke her heart.

Crystal rolls her eyes and sighs. "*Fine.* See you guys later, then."

I look back into Grace's hazel eyes, wondering if this will be the last time I'll get to see them. Before I get a chance to say anything, a shock of platinum blond hair and bright red lips burst into my field of view.

"*Austin!*" A hyperfeminine voice squeals in delight. Mary-Beth throws herself onto me and balances on her tiptoes tryin' to kiss my neck.

"Mary-Beth, what the hell are you doin'?" I pull her off me as my eyes flash to Grace. She touches her neck as she turns away.

"Just trying to give you a kiss," Mary-Beth says.

41

"Well, don't," I say.

Mary-Beth is dressed like one of those old-school pinup girls. She's a smokeshow, alright. But I find myself more attracted to Grace's natural down-to-earth style. Stepping back, I try to put some distance between me and Mary-Beth. Looking up, I see that Grace and Crystal are already walking away.

"Grace," I call out. I say it a bit more forcefully than I mean to. She stops and looks back at me. "See you around."

"Bye, Austin." She looks at me one last time before pulling away.

Looking back at Mary-Beth, I shake my head.

"What the hell, Mary-Beth?" I touch my neck. "I told ya not to do that anymore."

"You didn't mind it a few weeks ago when we were neckin' in my mama's car!" As she speaks, the silver 'M' charm on her necklace lodges in the crack of her plump cleavage.

I wipe the gunk off my neck. "You always leave orange stuff all over my collar."

"It's called foundation."

"Lipstick too, if you wanna get technical about it."

She sighs. "Can't a girl kiss her boyfriend?"

Joe looks at me. "Boyfriend?"

He knows I've been having trouble with Mary-Beth ever since Ma set us up on a blind date earlier this summer.

I sigh. "I'm not your boyfriend, Mary-Beth. I made that clear last time we talked."

"Why not?" Her wide eyes could break a puppy's heart. "I thought we had something!"

42

People are starting to stop and watch. Rubbing the back of my head, I look around at all the curious faces. I notice that Grace is long gone now.

Letting out a heavy sigh, I close my eyes and pinch the bridge of my nose. "We went on a few dates, Mary-Beth. That's it. I'm leavin' in two days, anyway."

"So?" She stands a bit taller, pushing out her chest slightly. "Seattle ain't that far."

I lower my voice. "Let's not do this here, okay?"

"Then, when? You wanna fight at your party? Huh?"

"I don't wanna fight at all! Plenty of guys would be lucky to date you."

"Wrong answer. If this is how you wanna do it, then I'll make it a party you'll *never* forget." She huffs before stomping away in her jean shorts and bright red heels.

I let out a heavy sigh as I turn to Joe.

"That's still going on?" He asks.

Dragging my hand through my hair, I shake my head. "I don't know. We went on three of the most boring dates in history. I don't know why she keeps wantin' more."

Joe chuckles. "I don't know, man... you ain't funny and you definitely ain't handsome. But you're rich as hell. That's gotta keep a woman interested. I know from firsthand experience."

Shaking my head, I clap him on the shoulder. "Thanks for the confidence boost, buddy."

Looking in the other direction, I continue scanning the crowd for Grace.

"You okay?" Joe asks.

"Yeah, just tired, I guess. The last day of Applelooza is always the most exhausting."

"Don't forget to save some energy for the party. You'll need it if Hurricane Mary-Beth shows up."

"If this is gonna be one of your crazy parties, Mary-Beth will be the least of my worries."

"Oh, it will be."

I clear my throat. "Did you find out if Grace is gonna show up at the party tomorrow?"

"No clue," he says. "Come on, man. Let's get to the convention center before all the good seats are taken."

Lost in my thoughts, I follow him through the crowd.

— 5 —

GRACE

"*Damn!*" Crystal laughs. "Are you okay? You pulled out of there faster than a college boy without a condom."

"I'm fine," I lie.

The chaos of the carnival closes in around us as I lead Crystal toward the Tilt-A-Whirl and as far away from Austin Berr as possible. I can't believe I kissed him *again*. It's the world's worst deja-vu. Do I have no control around him?

It might be because he's just as handsome as ever. Being around him reminds me of why I kissed him in the first place. He's still got that southern charm that makes me weak in the knees. And he's got those sparkling blue eyes and those delicious pillowy lips. But he doesn't respond to any of my advances. Not six years ago, and not now. It's the same old nightmare.

See you around? What did that even mean? Does he want to see me again before he leaves? Or is he just being polite to his best friend's silly little sister? Ugh. This is my least favorite carnival game.

"Are you *sure* you're okay?" Crystal asks, pulling me back to the present moment. My belly clenches.

"Was that Austin's girlfriend?" I ask. I try to prevent my voice from shaking.

Crystal scrunches her nose as she squints and scans the crowd. "Mary-Beth? They went on a couple of dates. But she's been datin' a lot of other guys this summer too. That girl goes down faster than these rides the day after Applelooza."

"Oh…"

Great. So, Austin will sleep with her but he won't kiss me. I guess that clears things up.

Crystal narrows her gaze. "Can you just admit you like him? It'll be a lot easier to talk about this stuff if you do."

I look around at the people walking past us. The smell of popcorn wafts through the air. The sun is starting to descend and small clouds of tiny flies are dancing in the pink sky.

"Fine," I say. "I kissed him."

Her eyes grow wide. "*What?* When?"

"Just now, in the haunted house."

"Holy shit." She pulls me closer, making sure we're not on the path anymore. "Tell me everything."

I shake my head. "There's nothing to tell. I kissed him and he didn't kiss me back. It's that simple."

Tale as old as time.

"Oh, honey." She gives me a hug and strokes my hair. "At least we know that he didn't want Mary-Beth either."

"So, we *do* have something in common." I let out a sad chuckle.

46

Crystal laughs. "Compared to Mary-Beth, you're a fuckin' angel."

Sirens and pinging noises come from the carnival games nearby. I can smell cotton candy and onion rings as people walk by with food.

"It's his loss anyway," Crystal says. "He's just a big dummy who doesn't know what he's missing."

I shake my head. "I don't know why I care anyway. It's not like I'm looking for male companionship or anything. That's the last thing I need right now."

"Ah, unrequited young love… it hurts like a bitch."

"It's not love," I say. "It's just… it's nothing."

Crystal watches me wistfully. "Come on, girl. Let's get more churros and watch hot cowboys do tricks."

"Oh, alright. You've convinced me." I smirk at her as we make our way to the arena.

After several hours of watching rodeo tricks with Crystal and Brad, I say goodbye and make my way through my old neighborhood back to the house. The sun is setting and the temperature is dropping. Although the rodeo was fun and the cinnamon churro was delicious, they could only do so much to dampen how mortified I still feel over today's events. It's hard to fault myself when every emotion feels heightened around Austin. He brings back so many feelings from the past. It's hard not to indulge in them, even just a little. After all, he was my first crush. And he lives up to my memory of him.

Once I'm in bed, I will myself to sleep. My eyelids are heavy and my brain feels like mush but I can't sleep. I stare up at the glow-in-the-dark stars stuck on my ceiling. I remember getting them for my thirteenth birthday. I stare at them for what feels like hours. It's hard to turn off my brain when I can't stop thinking about Austin.

When I finally fall asleep, I dream that I'm floating through the clouds. The dreamy sky fades away and I see Austin standing in the hellish red light from the haunted roller coaster ride. The red light washes everything out except his crystal-clear blue eyes. Just like earlier, he's unreadable. I step closer but he pulls back. I jerk awake.

Disoriented, I blink into the darkness. I look around, allowing my eyes to adjust to the darkness so that I can figure out where I am. The clock on the dresser is the only source of light. It's one o'clock. It's the middle of the night but I feel fully rested. It should be around noon in Thailand. At this time of the day, I'd be finishing a shift at the local shelter and joining my exercise buddies for yoga on the beach.

Rolling out of bed, I bump into a few walls before remembering that I'm in my childhood room. Making my way down the hall to the washroom, I wash my face and look in the mirror. I've looked into this mirror a thousand times but I feel like a completely different woman now. There's no more baby fat on these cheeks, and I look wild... not just because my hair is disheveled but because my eyes have seen all sorts of things. Wonderful things, horrible things... things I wish I could unsee. I stare at myself until I don't recognize my reflection. Feeling uneasy, I pull away.

My mouth feels like sandpaper so I head downstairs to get a glass of water. The house is dark and quiet. I can't tell if Joe is sleeping in the master bedroom upstairs or down in the basement like he used to back in high school. Either way, I tiptoe through the living room, avoiding the creaky floorboards just like I did when I was a teenager. I make my way to the kitchen where the only light is coming from the hood of the stove. Grabbing a glass of water, I drink it all at once and let out a satisfied sigh. Re-filling my glass, I do it again. A door opens behind me. It's the basement door—I recognize that squeak.

"Joe?" I turn.

"No," a deep voice says. "It's Austin."

His large silhouette appears in the doorway. He's in the same t-shirt and jeans as earlier. He looks a bit dustier now after spending all day at Applelooza. I'm highly aware that I'm only wearing silk pajama shorts and a tank top.

"What are you doing here?" I ask. My mouth suddenly feels dry again.

"Joe and I hung out after the concert. He was pretty drunk so I drove him home. He's passed out downstairs."

"You're not drunk?"

He smirks. "No, but I'm just as clueless as ever."

His boyish charm comes through.

Slightly amused, I lean back against the counter. "I guess now that you're a professional athlete, you don't drink very much."

"You'd be surprised. It's hard keepin' up with some of the guys back in Seattle."

"Maybe you should bring them some of that grapefruit moonshine you love. I know you can drink anyone under the table when moonshine's involved."

He rubs his chin. "That's actually a good idea."

"I have some of those sometimes."

He smiles as he stares into my eyes. The silence lingers for a bit too long. I pull my gaze away. I know we're both thinking about that awkward kiss from earlier.

"Well... thanks for bringing Joe back home in one piece," I say. "I don't know how he survives without you."

"Heh. That's a mystery to me too. By the way, there's some apple pie in the fridge for you. It was the contest winner."

I raise my brows. "You brought some back for me?"

"You can't come to Applelooza and *not* have apple pie."

"Wow, that's so nice of you. Thanks for thinking of me."

After dealing with selfish guys for the past few years, it's nice to remember what a nice guy is actually like.

"Hey," he says, chuckling to himself. "Remember when we went to Applelooza together that one summer? I was supposed to go with you and Joe—"

"—but Joe bailed. Yeah, I remember. That was the first time you and I spent the day alone together."

"That's right. Remember the Mars exhibit?"

I smile. "Yeah."

He chuckles. "You said you'd never go to Mars because there was no ocean there. And you loved swimmin' in the ocean way too much to give it up."

Astonished, I stare at him. "You remember that?"

"Dang right, I remember. Every time I see the ocean now, I make sure to swim in it."

"You really do that?"

"Hell yeah. I even swim in Seattle where the water is cold enough to freeze your balls off. Well... *my* balls off. Those Martians don't know what they're missin'."

I laugh. "I can't believe you remember that."

His piercing blue eyes watch me. "I remember lots of things about you, Grace."

The sound of my name on his lips makes my belly fill with butterflies. I can't help myself when he says my name-my *real* name.

50

His gaze lingers. The hum of the fridge fills the room, reminding me that we're standing in the middle of the kitchen in the middle of the night. The stove light casts a dim light over him, highlighting his strong jaw, his pink cheeks, and the rest of his boyish good looks. Alone with him here, I realize just how massive he is. There's a reason why the hockey world calls him The Bear.

"I should go back to bed," I say, highly aware that he's standing between me and my way out.

"Why?" He asks. "Afraid you might kiss me again?"

A flood of heat rushes to my cheeks. I didn't realize he'd bring that up so bluntly. His piercing blue eyes hold me in place.

"That was a mistake," I say. "A silly mistake."

"You did it twice."

I expect to see some sort of self-satisfied smirk on his face but his expression is curious and unmoving. His eyes are laser-focused on me.

"Yeah... I guess I make a lot of silly mistakes. I'm Graceless, right?" I try to laugh it off.

"No," he says in a serious tone. "This is the second time you kiss me right before I'm about to leave."

I shake my head. "I didn't plan that."

He exhales breathily and lowers his voice. "What are you doin' to me, Grace?"

I've never heard him talk to me in this voice before. "I'm not trying to do anything to you."

"Have you been hidin' from me?"

"No! That's ridiculous."

"Then what are you hidin' from?" His eyes search mine.

I pull back against the counter. "Why do you think I'm hiding at all?"

"I know you, Grace. You moved a lot when you were young. You liked it… movin' meant you could disappear and become a new person. You told me that once."

"So?"

"You left Tennessee and disappeared… now I'm wonderin', did you become a new person? Or are you the same old Grace?"

I casually shrug a shoulder. "What does it matter?"

His careful eyes watch me. "Because I'm curious."

Lifting my chin, I look him in the eyes. "We're both different people now."

A lonely train sounds its horn in the distance. I can feel just how close Austin and I are in this small kitchen.

"You should go home." I avert his gaze. "It's late."

"No," he says. "I wanna clear some things up between us."

"There's nothing to talk about."

He takes a step closer. "I think there is."

"Fine." I look up at him. "I'm sorry, okay? Is that what you want to hear? I'm sorry that I find you so annoyingly and irresistibly attractive that I kissed you. *Twice*. I wish I had better self-control, but I don't. I never did. Sometimes I get robbed in Thailand, and sometimes I kiss my brother's best friend. I'm a flawed person and I make bad decisions sometimes. Is that better? Is that what you wanted me to say?"

My raised voice echoes through the kitchen as I stop to catch my breath. If Joe is drunk and passed out downstairs, he won't hear us.

I avoid Austin's gaze. "I'll never tell anyone and it'll never happen again."

"It'll never happen again?"

52

"Yeah, isn't that what you want? You can say you don't like me. It won't hurt my feelings. I get the gist."

He furrows his brow. "Don't like you?"

He steps closer, backing me up against the kitchen counter. My mouth falls open as I look up into his impossibly blue eyes. His wide shoulders block out the dim light.

"You think I don't like you? Grace... I've been thinking about you for *six* years."

Time slows as I process his words. "Wh—what?"

"Didn't you notice that I spent more time in high school with you than with my girlfriend? Hell, you were the first person I told when I broke up with her!"

"You came over to hang out with Joe."

"I came to your house every Thursday even though I knew Joe had karate lessons on Thursday nights. You must've noticed."

"I thought you were just forgetful."

His lips curl into a subtle smile. "I am. But I do have *some* sense in that brain of mine. Grace... I've spent the next six years comparin' every woman I dated to you, and I still haven't found someone like you."

"You mean you can't find any women who will spend hours talking about the water content on Mars?" Humor is my attempt to diffuse the sizzling tension but it's no use. I can feel his heat sparking in the air between us.

He chuckles. "Among other things."

"Like what?"

"The things we talk about, your values..."

"My values?" I laugh. "I'm an agnostic feminist who sleeps with strangers and doesn't want to get married."

"Sure… but you care about people. You volunteer to help the less fortunate. And you're open to learnin' about other cultures and opinions. Plus, you care about hockey."

"It wasn't the hockey that I cared about."

"And that's why I liked you."

I look up into his eyes. The tension between us is palpable. "Why didn't you ever tell me?"

He shakes his head. "I had the pieces but I didn't put the puzzle together 'til you kissed me. And before I figured it out, it was over. You were gone. I went on a lot of dates thinking I'd connect with someone as easily as I connected with you. But I never did. And now you're here and we're connectin' just like we used to. And you're kissin' me again…"

My heart is racing. "If you feel that way, why won't you kiss me back?"

"Trust me, I want to…"

I'm acutely aware of how close he is. "You do?"

"Yes, ma'am." He stares at my lips.

"So, why won't you?" I whisper.

"I'm done with mindless hookups and one-night stands," he says. "And I don't wanna kiss you unless it's serious."

"Not even this one night?" I place a hand on his chest.

"Not even this one night," he repeats, pulling my hand from his chest. His hands are so large, so warm. Lifting one of them, he strokes my cheek. "I'm warnin' ya, if I start kissin' you, it's over, I won't be able to stop."

The corners of my lips pull up into a subtle smile. "You say that like it's a bad thing."

He smirks. "It ain't a bad thing. But when I say I won't be able to stop, I ain't talkin' about sex… I'm talkin' about everything. Sex, love, marriage, babies, dogs… would that be bad for you?"

I stay quiet.

"Because if I remember correctly," he continues, "back in high school, you told me you never wanted to get married. You said you just wanna travel the world forever. And it seems like you get what you wish for."

"What are we doing?" I ask. "Playing games?"

"That's what I'm tryin' to figure out." He places his hands on either side of me as he leans on the counter behind me, locking me in his space. "You know exactly what I want."

Heat pounds through my body. Is he really saying all this right now?

"Are you seriously saying you won't kiss me unless I agree to marry you?" I ask. "Or is this a jet lag and sugar-induced hallucination?"

He chuckles. "That's not what I'm sayin'… I just don't want to kiss you if there's no future for us."

His eyes look into mine. I see the sincerity.

"I don't want just one night with you," he says. "I want every night with you."

I swallow. My throat feels dry again. I shake my head and look away. "You're such a hypocrite."

He laughs in disbelief. "Why?"

Reaching out, I touch the small gold cross hanging around his neck. "I know you're not the perfect church-going man that your mom thinks you are. I know you're not a virgin."

Smirking, he tucks the cross under his shirt.

"And I know you had casual sex with Mary-Beth."

"That's not true," he says. "I kissed her but we didn't have sex. Ain't nothin' casual about sex."

55

"You kissed her but you won't kiss me?"

He pauses as he looks into my eyes. "You're different."

"Why? Because I'm Joe's little sister?"

He thinks for a moment. "Sorta, yeah."

"What does that matter?"

"Because if I kiss you, you'll have to see me every time you come back to Tennessee—that's every Christmas, every Easter, every summer... could you handle that? Or would you keep hidin' from me?"

I shake my head. "I'm not hiding."

"Do you still wanna kiss me, then? Because I'll kiss you right now if you're ready for the consequences."

I blink a few times. My lips are pulsing. My heart is beating. This is the moment I've been dreaming of since high school. Austin Berr is confessing that he has feelings for me. That he's been thinking about me all these years. *That he wants a future with me.* But getting into a relationship with him? Having to settle down and give up my life? I've never wanted anything serious, not after witnessing my mom's trainwreck of a marriage. Happy endings aren't so common in the real world... not when it comes to men, anyway.

Austin is probably the only man who could convince me otherwise. There's just something about him that draws me in, even after all these years.

"I don't wanna go another six years without seeing you," he says. "I ain't gonna make that mistake again. And I won't let you break my heart, Grace Lawless. One night with you ain't enough because once I get a taste of you, I won't want anyone else."

His southern accent does things to me.

"Tell me you won't hide from me," he says in a whisper. My heart pounds as those icy blue eyes watch my lips, lusting after them. "Say the word and I'll be your protector."

56

"You won't kiss me until we're in a relationship?" I blink up at him. "A *real* relationship that ends with marriage and babies and going on lots of cruises once we're old?"

He chuckles. "The cruises are optional. I prefer road trips down to the beach."

The idea of a road trip to the beach with Austin sounds tempting. Meanwhile, my throat is constricting at the thought of any long-term commitment.

I shake my head. "I can't respond to any of that right now."

He watches me as if he's studying me. "You'll kiss me, but you won't go on a date with me?"

"I—"

The basement door squeaks and my brother hauls himself up the last few stairs and into the kitchen. Austin pulls away, leaving me feeling cold in his absence. Joe looks around the room. His hair is messy and his eyes are heavy. He burps loudly, causing the strong scent of beer to fill the room and sting deep in my nostrils.

"Ew." I fan the air.

"Any pie left?" He asks, completely ignoring the fact that Austin and I are in the kitchen together at nearly two in the morning.

"No," Austin says.

Joe opens the fridge. "Liar. There's some right here."

"That's for Grace." Austin's eyes connect with mine.

I stare at him for a moment. "It's fine. I've lost my appetite anyway."

"Sweet." Joe starts eating right there with the fridge open.

"Excuse me." I head for the door.

"Grace." Austin tries to get me to stop but I ignore him.

Rushing out of the kitchen, I avoid the squeaky floorboards as I make my way back up to my room. Sitting on my bed, I press my palms against my eyes. This is all too much to process.

Austin *wants* me? And he doesn't just want a hookup. He wants the whole fucking thing. The idea of giving up my independence and becoming a good little wife doesn't sit right with me. Why can't Austin be like every other normal horndog guy in his twenties? Why does he have to bring real relationship stuff into this when we could be in the middle of a mindless makeout session right now? Annoyed, I lean back on my bed and stare up at the glow-in-the-dark stars.

I've never wanted to be in a relationship and I'm not gonna start now. I saw how marriage ruined my mom's life and she carried that stress until she died. I'm not signing away my life for Austin. I don't care that I've been pining for him since high school. I'm an independent woman. I live life on my terms, not his.

— 6 —

AUSTIN

My birthday starts before sunrise when I join Pa for a drive around the farm. We use the small helicopter that I bought for him last year. It used to take him over forty-five minutes of driving around the property to check on everything. With the helicopter, he can do it in ten minutes. I never discussed it with him. I simply landed in his backyard one day and handed him the keys. He said it was overkill but after one ride, he was hooked. Riding the helicopter is his favorite part of the day. As he steers us around the property, we watch the sunrise cast orange light over the vast fields. The cows scatter below, running in all directions as we pass by.

"Another trip around the sun, huh?" Pa looks out the window.

"That's right," I say. "Twenty-four years old. I'm not feelin' so young anymore."

"Any goals this year?"

Pa has always been obsessed with goals. I think that's the reason I've always been so driven and disciplined.

"I don't know. Work's goin' alright. I've got my new condo waitin' for me back in Seattle. I guess I'll have to think of some goals."

"You as happy at work as you could be?"

I exhale. "Maybe I could be better. I'm the muscle of the team but I ain't gettin' any younger. These new guys are bigger, stronger, and more skilled. It's rough."

"Make yourself useful in other ways," he says in his gruff voice.

"What, like get better at scorin'?"

"That's right," Pa says. "You're never tied to one choice. Remember that."

I nod. "Thanks for the advice, Pa."

"And what about a family?" Pa asks. "You seein' anyone?"

I've been in Tennessee all summer and this is the first time he's asking this? That's Pa in a nutshell.

"No, I'm not."

"Better look for a wife. You need support."

I laugh. "I've got plenty of money."

"Not that kind of support. You need someone who will make you smile when you're sad. You need someone who will believe in you when you don't believe in yourself." He coughs. "Your Ma and I ain't gonna be here forever. I wanna know you'll be in good hands."

It's rare for Pa to be this open. I reach over and squeeze his shoulder. "Thanks, Pa."

"How about another fly-by, before headin' in?"

After another ten minutes in the helicopter, we make our way inside for breakfast. Ma has the kitchen table all set up

60

with everything we could possibly want—pancakes, scrambled eggs, bacon, and coffee. It's been good being home.

"I'm sure gonna miss this," I say, pouring fresh milk into my coffee.

"You've been inside for two minutes and you're already on your second coffee!" Ma is still in her nightgown, standing over the table and watching over everything, making sure we have enough food. We always have enough food.

"I'm tired." I sip on the piping hot coffee.

"Because you were out late last night," she says. I can't tell if that's an accusation or a question.

"I was with Joe. We went to the Katy Ray concert." I shove a forkful of eggs into my mouth so that I won't have to explain any further. I was up late because I was chattin' with Grace, but that's my secret. The conversation I had with her was surreal. The tension between us just kept escalating. I was tempted as hell to kiss her but I refuse to kiss her and leave her. That's not my style. Grace Lawless deserves more than that.

"We were at the Katy Ray concert too," Ma says. "We weren't out that late!"

"Give it a rest, Shelby," Pa says. "The boy's allowed to stay out late. It's his birthday."

"I just want him to be ready for hockey in a few days."

"I'll be fine," I say. "I'll make sure to resist Joe's negative influence."

Pa laughs and chokes on a piece of bacon.

"Why are you laughing?" Ma puts a hand on her hip. She's got a dish towel in her hand and I know she's ready to smack Pa with it any second.

"You never liked that Lawless boy, admit it," Pa says.

61

"I do like him! He's just… bless his heart, but he's always been a bit reckless." She pokes at the strips of bacon still cooking on the stove.

I chuckle. "Joe's doin' alright now, ain't he?"

"Cleaned up my truck real good the other day." Pa sits back and sips on a black cup of coffee.

"I guess he's okay," Ma mumbles.

Pa and I smirk at each other as I load more scrambled eggs onto my plate.

"Did you hear about his sister?" Ma asks.

I perk up. "Grace? What about her?"

"She's back. Apparently, she got robbed in Thailand."

Gossip sure travels fast.

"I saw her yesterday," I say. "She seems to be doin' okay."

"The poor girl," Ma continues. "First, she had to deal with that horrible father. And then her mom died while she was still in high school… she can't catch a break."

"You have sympathy for the girl, but not her brother?" Pa asks. He sips his coffee as if he's hiding behind his mug.

"I have sympathy for both of them!" Ma says. "But at least Joe made something of himself. Grace is just… lost. She left her only family member behind and she's just drifting through life aimlessly…"

My temperature is starting to rise. I drop the piece of bacon back onto my plate.

"Grace Lawless is an interesting and compassionate person," I say. "She spends her time volunteerin' for different churches and shelters in foreign countries. And just because she doesn't make money or have a job title doesn't mean she's lost."

"Hmmph." Pa crunches into another slice of bacon. "She volunteers, she doesn't care about money... she sounds better than most of the young women at the church."

Ma's cheeks look red. "Well... I know those Lawless siblings aren't religious, but I pray she's happy. Anyone who has gone through so much tragedy and still has a kind heart deserves some sort of peace. Especially a young woman with no parents and no children. A woman like that needs a good purpose to keep her going. I hope she has it. And if she doesn't, I hope she finds it."

Staring at the eggs on my plate, I think about everything Grace and Joe have been through. I've heard the stories about their abusive dad and I knew their mom, Jill, before she died. But it takes moments like these for me to realize just how privileged I am to still have my parents around, to still have a loving home to go to on Christmas. Joe and Grace will always be my family, and I know Joe considers me part of his. Grace on the other hand... maybe Ma's right. Maybe Grace is lost.

A horn honks outside. I recognize the sound—it's Joe's truck.

"Speak of the devil," Pa says.

"Party startin' already?" Ma looks around with raised eyebrows.

"It's Joe," I say, getting up from the table. "He ain't wastin' time when it comes to partyin', not when it's my last day here."

Ma sighs. "Of course, he's not!"

I eat the last strip of bacon and down the rest of my coffee. "I'll join you for tomorrow morning's helicopter ride, Pa."

"No," he says. "Not after the big party. I want you to enjoy yourself and sleep in."

"I'll at least be back to drive Ma to church."

"We're *all* going to church tomorrow," Ma says. "And then we're having a big lunch before driving you to the airport."

"Gotta be out of here by noon," Pa says. "Takes twenty minutes to get to Memphis International."

"So, don't get too crazy at the party."

"Let the boy have fun, Shelby!"

Ma sighs. "I don't want him getting all comfortable now that he's rich and famous! He needs to set a good example for the young kids."

My parents bicker for a moment as I chuckle to myself. I'm definitely gonna miss this.

Ma shuffles around the table and kisses me on the cheek. "Have fun and happy birthday."

"Thanks, Ma."

Pa nods at me. I nod back.

Pulling on my boots, I head outside. Joe's red pickup truck is in the driveway. Joe is hanging out the driver's side window. His shaggy hair is messy as usual but he's got dark circles around his eyes.

"Damn, you look rough," I say. "You look like you've been tossed around by one of them bulls over at the Applelooza rodeo."

"I'm hungover as hell." He winces in the sunlight. "Why did we decide to drink after last night's concert again?"

I laugh. "That was your idea, Joe."

"Right." He runs a hand through his messy hair. "You know what the solution is then, right?"

"More drinkin'?"

"Hell yeah, more drinkin'." He taps the side of his truck. "Get in. We're wastin' precious party time."

"Alright, you don't have to tell me twice."

Joe drives as he whistled along to a country song playing on the radio. I'm in my good jeans, my best button-down, and my cowboy boots. I wasn't gonna dress this nice but if I'm gonna be seein' Grace, I want to look somewhat presentable. At least I've got my teeth in this time.

"Ma wants me to go to church tomorrow mornin'," I say. "So, I might not stay too late. Maybe midnight."

"Are you kiddin'?" Joe looks over. "I don't want you sobering up and leaving before midnight! That's right when things get good."

"In my experience, it's the exact opposite. Midnight is when mistakes start happenin'."

"Good mistakes."

I laugh. "Agree to disagree."

"What's that smell?" Joe asks.

"What, my cologne? I was wearin' it yesterday."

"It smells stronger today."

"You like it?"

Joe's nostrils flare as he inhales. "Yeah, I do."

"It's called Dark Rodeo."

"You tryin' to impress someone?"

"Uhm—no." I swallow.

"Because there'll be lots of girls there tonight. I don't know about the whole Mary-Beth situation but you won't be lonely tonight."

Right. Mary-Beth. I forgot about her. All it took was seeing Grace again to wipe her from my mind. I won't be surprised if Mary-Beth shows up tonight. Grace on the other hand? I don't know. She has a habit of disappearing.

I clear my throat. "Grace gonna be there?"

I realize how fucking obvious it is to ask that when we're talking about women. Luckily, Joe is too hungover to connect the dots.

Joe half-shrugs. "Hell if I know. Haven't seen her yet today."

Hiding again? Not surprising.

"Why do you care?" Joe asks.

"Didn't get much time to talk to her yesterday." My palms feel sweaty. "I wouldn't mind pickin' her brain about Thailand."

"Well, don't waste your night talking to Grace. One of the girls who works at my car wash is in a sorority and she's bringing some friends."

I acknowledge him with a grunt. I don't really care about sorority girls. As long as I can talk to Grace about last night, then my birthday wish will be granted.

It only takes ten minutes to get to the Lawless house. Walking in, I notice everything is spotless.

"There's no way you cleaned this place," I say.

Joe laughs. "Naw, my cleaning lady came by."

"Shoulda waited to bring her in tomorrow. I'm sure the place will look like a zoo."

"Don't worry, I've got that covered too."

Looking into the living room, I see a table with large glass drink jugs.

"Sangria, mojitos, beer—it's everything you could possibly want," Joe says.

"And a poker table." I walk over to the green-felted table. Poker chips and cards are neatly organized on the table, waiting to be played. "Sweet."

Playing poker with the guys on the team has made me slightly better. I'm curious to see how my new skills hold up against guys from Tennessee.

"And check out the backyard," Joe says. I follow him through the kitchen and stand at the door looking out toward the backyard. Although the Lawless family is one of the few without a farm, they still have a large backyard property. Big speakers sit on either side of the house. A few coolers and a snack table are set up by the door. I see cornhole boards and bean bags, tables, lawn chairs, and a few trucks parked nearby.

I squint. "Is that a hot tub in the back of that truck?"

Joe nods as he eyes the truck greedily. "Hell yeah, buddy."

"Dang!"

"Remember when I mentioned the sorority girls?" He pats me on the back. "You can thank me later."

"I don't know what to say."

"Happy birthday, buddy." He squeezes my shoulder.

There's a shuffling sound in the house behind us. I turn and see Grace in the kitchen. She freezes like a deer caught in the headlights.

"Grace," Joe says. "Did you pick up the ice?"

Grace's eyes dart between me and her brother.

"Was I supposed to?" She asks. She's wearing an old baggy school shirt and black leggings.

He exhales heavily. "I texted you."

"I don't have a phone, genius," she says. "It was stolen in Thailand, remember?"

"Oh, yeah," Joe says sheepishly. "Okay… well, I need ice."

"I'd be a lot more inclined to obey your orders if you said please."

He huffs loudly. "I said please in the text!"

"The text I never got."

I chuckle. "It's good to know that the Lawless sibling rivalry is alive and well."

They ignore me. It's the same thing they would've done a decade ago.

"It's fine," I say, attempting to de-escalate the situation. "I'll pick up the ice."

They look at me.

"I don't want Grace doin' chores for me," I say.

Her hazel eyes find mine. "No, I'll do it. But only because it's Austin's birthday. *Not* because of you, Joe."

She shoots a scornful look at her brother.

Joe exhales again. "Good. Now that we got that sorted out, let's pick up more beer. Come on, Austin."

He heads toward the back entrance.

"I'll meet you out there in a minute," I say.

"Don't keep me waitin'." Joe steps out the back entrance to the backyard.

Grace and I are now alone in the kitchen. She'd got one foot in the kitchen and one foot out. She eyes the exit but I know she won't leave. Not until her curiosity is satisfied.

"You're doing somethin' nice for me on my birthday?"

"Yeah… it's your birthday. Why wouldn't I?" She raises her chin. "You thought I'd hide again?"

I smirk. "I never know what you're gonna do. I think that's why I'm so intrigued."

She smiles. "I *can* meet halfway so that we can coexist and be friendly."

"So, is that what we are? Friends?"

She looks up with those big vulnerable eyes. Her voice softens. "You'll always be a friend."

"*Just* a friend?"

Keeping her gaze, I feel the tension in the air between us.

She raises her brows. "Are asking me to be your girlfriend again?"

"Is that what I did yesterday?"

"Umm… I'm pretty sure."

I see the tiniest smirk on her lips. She's enjoying this little game.

"Why do we always end up in the kitchen?" I ask. "Maybe I should pick a more romantic spot next time."

"Maybe you should ask me later by the hot tub when the sorority girls are watching."

I chuckle. "I'd hope I could organize somethin' nicer than that."

"Nicer than beer kegs and tailgating? I don't think that exists out here."

She's cute. *Real* cute. And I can't stop staring at her. It's blatant enough that I can tell she notices. She's got that subtle smile where she keeps lookin' away, almost like she's embarrassed, but then she looks back up at me with those big hazel eyes and that innocent smile. Gosh, she's cute.

She watches me with an amused expression as if she's reading my thoughts. A squeak nearby grabs my attention. Someone is standing in the hallway. It's Crystal in a bright red sun dress.

"Sorry," she says. "Didn't mean to intrude."

"Oh." Grace clears her throat. "I'm just wrapping up over here."

"You guys okay?" She asks.

"Yeah, I'm just leaving. We need to go get some ice."

"Alright." She pulls away down the hall.

Grace's hazel eyes flash at me one last time before she pulls away too.

"Will I see you tonight?" I ask.

She pauses and looks back. "Maybe… have a good birthday, Austin."

I smirk. "Thanks, Grace."

She pulls on her lip and stares at me for a moment as if the sound of her name unlocked something in her. Finally, she pulls away. Once she's gone, I realize that my heart is racing. I head outside and get some fresh air as I join Joe in the red truck.

I stand by what I said to Grace last night. I'm done with modern datin'. No one-night stands, no hookups. I know what I want. And I ain't backin' down.

— 7 —

GRACE

After spending the day with Crystal and picking up ice on the way home, we hang out in my bedroom. She's standing at the dresser while I sit on the bed and demolish a bag of potato chips. There's already trap music playing over the speakers in the backyard.

"I don't know why Joe has the music on already," I say. "It's only seven o'clock."

"I can't believe Austin wants to date you!" Crystal's been changing the subject back to me and Austin all day. I couldn't keep last night's conversation a secret from her, especially not after she caught us flirting in the kitchen.

"Doesn't matter. Nothing's gonna happen."

"You don't think so?" She's pulling open the dresser drawers, searching through my old high school clothes.

"I know so. He's leaving tomorrow."

"So?"

"He doesn't want a one-night hookup."

71

Crystal looks at me expectantly. *"So?"*

I shrug. "What else am I supposed to do?"

"Actually *try* going on a date with him? Maybe?"

The scenario plays out in my mind for half a second before I shake my head. "I didn't think my faith in men could fall any further but that Thailand robbery? Well, it pushed me over the edge."

"You don't think Austin's different than other men?" She pulls a yellow dress out of the bottom drawer.

"I have yet to meet a man who hasn't let me down."

"Oh, hon. You've had a rough ride, haven't you?"

"A rough ride... that's one way of putting it."

"Don't let it harden you. I want you to relax and treat yourself." She looks into my eyes. "Maybe you need this."

"Treat myself how? By dating Austin?" I laugh. "That's not a treat. It's a defeat."

"Oh, you and your feminist rah-rah-rah bull-crap."

My mouth falls open in shock. "You don't believe in feminism?"

"I believe in equal rights for men and women, sure... but I don't think you should deprive yourself of having an intimate relationship with a man you've had a crush on for nearly ten years!"

I sigh and eat another potato chip.

"Don't you enjoy hangin' out with him?" She asks.

My memories flash back to last night when we were talking about Applelooza and Martians missing the ocean. Crunching on more chips, I smile as the memory plays out in my mind.

"I guess..."

"And don't you like the way he looks at you?" Crystal is looking in the full-length mirror, holding up the yellow dress to see how it'll fit.

I sit up. "How does he look at me?"

She smiles at me through the reflection. "Like he never wants to look away."

Is that true? I've been so overwhelmed and confused by everything over the past few days. I still can't tell what's real and what's a result of jet lag and sleep deprivation.

"What would you do?" I ask.

"If a rich, successful, *sexy* hockey player said he wanted a future with me? To protect me for the rest of time?"

"Yeah..." I have a sense that I already know her answer.

She turns and faces me. "I would melt into a puddle at his feet faster than a popsicle on the fourth of July. He's got real king energy. *And* he's got nice hands."

I laugh. "Nice hands?"

"Yeah. If a guy has well-kept hands, you know he takes care of himself. When I see clean, well-kept fingernails, I can't help it. I wanna see what else those fingers can do."

I smirk. "I can't say I noticed his hands."

Except when they were on my waist when we were in the haunted house.

"The fact that it's Austin on top of all that? That's just icin' on the hunky cake," she continues. "He's one of the good ones."

"You think good ones exist?"

She raises her brows. "You don't?"

"Name a single relationship that has lasted."

"My Aunt Bessie and Uncle Cody."

I laugh. "Your Uncle Cody's been in jail for four years!"

73

"And Aunt Bessie has stood by him the entire time. That's true love if you ask me!"

I stifle my laughter. "Alright, who else?"

Crystal thinks for a moment. "Austin's parents. They celebrated their twenty-fifth anniversary this year."

I think about Austin's parents—Shelby and Norm. I met them a few times at birthdays and barbecues. They're kind, cheerful, and hardworking people. I can definitely tell that Austin got his goofy, friendly demeanor from them.

"Austin's parents would never accept me," I say. "I'm not a church-going girl."

"*Pfft*, who cares? The church-going girls here are little devils. You know Thora?"

"The girl who used to be in gym class with us?"

"That's right." Crystal leans in and lowers her voice. "She sells panties… *used* ones… on the internet."

"Wait… *what?*" That's not at all what I expected her to say. "Who buys those?"

She shrugs. "Lonely perverts with too much money."

"Oh…" I squeeze my eyes together and shake my head trying to figure out how the conversation got here. "I think I'd rather be broke."

There's laughter and chatter outside. Crystal and I look at each other before getting up and peeking out the window. The sun is low on the horizon but the lights are already on in the garden. About forty people are already in the backyard drinking and socializing. Cars and trucks are parked all over the lawn, including the pickup truck with the hot tub in the back. Two guys are already sitting in it. Others are dancing to the music. Austin's blond curls and massive height catch my attention. He's standing near the snack table, drinking beer, and chatting with a few guys from around the neighborhood. I mindlessly watch him.

74

Even if he's one of the good guys, is that what I want? I don't know how to be a girlfriend. I don't even know how to be a person. When I linger in a city for too long, people realize that I'm not as interesting as I pretend to be. When that happens, I simply pick up and leave. It's easier to give a good impression when I can start over from scratch. I don't know how to keep people interested over time. And I'm pretty sure I've got Austin fooled for the time being. He thinks I'm just as witty and mysterious as I was when I was a teenager—but I was faking it back then too. It would only take a few days for Austin to see through my facade. I'd prefer for him to pine after the fantasy of me rather than grow bored of the real thing.

"Earth to Grace." Crystal snaps her fingers in front of my face. "What are you thinkin' about?"

I blink and refocus my gaze. "I'm just wondering how to avoid this party tonight."

"Nuh-uh. We're definitely making an appearance."

"You're welcome to go right ahead," I say. "But I'd like to avoid watching Austin and my brother sit in a hot tub with a bunch of bikini-clad sorority girls… if that's okay with you."

"*Please* come! Please, please, *please*," she begs.

"I can't see him," I say. "It's too embarrassing."

"Embarrassing? What's embarrassing about a guy wanting to be in a committed relationship with you?"

"Things are just weird between us now. I don't know how to explain it."

Her shoulders collapse as she sighs. "Does this mean things are gonna be weird between you two forever?"

A pang of guilt radiates through my belly.

"I don't want them to be," I say.

75

This is exactly what Austin was warning me about. If we ever had a one-night stand, we'd have to deal with the awkward consequences forever. But based on how I'm feeling now, it seems like we'll have to deal with the awkward consequences no matter what, even if nothing ever happens.

Crystal's phone pings.

"Brad's on his way," she says.

"The guy at Applelooza? You finally decided to tell him about the party?"

"Yeah, I think I like hanging out with him. And he's cute… right?"

"He makes you laugh," I say. Looking back out the window, I watch Austin talk to one of the guys from Sparkle and Shine. As if sensing that someone's watching him, he looks around before looking up at my window. For some reason, I assume the glare from the sunset means he won't be able to see me. But based on how his eyes are connecting with mine, I quickly realize I'm wrong. My heart beats loudly in my chest as I pull away. Turning from the window, I look at Crystal. She's already wearing the yellow dress and now she's putting on dangly bracelets.

"You coming?" She asks.

My heart is still pounding in my chest. I can't hide from Austin, not after I told him I wasn't hiding from him last night.

"Fine." I relax my shoulders. "But I'm only going for an hour, an hour and a half *max*. After that, I'm coming back up here, locking my door, and putting on my headphones."

Crystal grins. "If you say so."

I narrow my eyes. "Why do I have the feeling that you'll convince me to stay longer?"

"I promise I won't, cross my heart. If it's after nine o'clock and I can't find you, I swear I won't come lookin'."

76

I nod. "Good."

Crystal claps excitedly. "Yay!"

Rubbing my temples, I take a deep breath. "I need to mentally prepare for this."

"Let's dress you up and make you look hot so that Austin will reconsider his 'no hookup' rule." She pulls open the dresser drawer. "You've gotta have something in here."

Ten minutes later, I'm wearing a perfectly curated casual but sexy outfit. I've got a strappy black velvet top that shows off my black bra and the tattoo on my ribs—that's the sexy part. The casual part is the swishy floor-length skirt that reminds me of being overseas. It shows off the ankle bracelet I bought in Botswana. Besides my elephant pants, the ankle bracelet is the only souvenir from the last four years that wasn't stolen from me.

Skipping the makeup, I use my fingers to comb out the waves in my long dark hair. Stepping back, I admire my reflection in the mirror.

"You're lookin' good," Crystal says. "Damn! Look at that tan! Those Thai beaches treated you well."

"Yeah." I think about the beautiful Thai coastline—the salty water, the palm trees, the white-sand beaches. I smile to myself thinking about Austin talking about the Martians missing out on swimming in the ocean. I can't believe he swims in the ocean just because of that comment. Crazy boy.

Crystal and I make our way downstairs to the kitchen. We grab two cups of bourbon lemonade before slipping on our flip-flops and stepping out into the backyard. There are about fifty people in the backyard now and the party is raging. We're surrounded by music, chatter, laughter, and chaos. As the sun inches closer to the horizon, people get louder and rowdier.

"This is exactly what I wanted!" Crystal says gleefully.

I scan the crowd but I can't see Austin.

"Oh, look!" Crystal grabs my arm. "It's Brad!"

She pulls me across the backyard where Brad is standing with a tall skinny friend. His face lights up when he sees her.

"Brad! I'm so glad you came." Crystal hugs him. He whispers something in her ear and she giggles. I'm left standing awkwardly next to Brad's friend. He's got three long curly hairs on his chin. He looks down at me, not hiding the fact that he's looking down into my barely-there cleavage.

"I'm Jordie," he says in a nasal voice.

"Grace," I say curtly.

I look around at all the people. I'm sure more are coming.

"You from here?" Jordie asks.

"Sort of. I used to live here. I've been traveling."

"Wow, like... out of the country?"

"Yeah."

"You ever been below the equator?" He asks.

"Uh-huh." I cross my arms, instinctively touching my ribs.

"Interesting!" He rubs his three-haired chin. "What direction do toilets flush down there?"

I furrow my brow. "What?"

"The toilets... do they flush clockwise or counter-clockwise?"

"Is that a joke?"

"Absolutely not! Apparently, they flush differently based on where you are in relation to the equator."

"Umm... I honestly never paid attention to that."

"Aww, damn." He sighs. "One day I'll go down there and figure it out for myself."

Shaking my head in disbelief, I collect my thoughts. "You want to travel over the equator just to look into a toilet bowl?"

"Yep," he says proudly.

"Oh."

The conversation falls silent. I take a sip of my drink as I look around, scanning the area for Austin. He's usually so easy to spot since he towers over everyone, but I can't see him. I look over at the hot tub but he's not there either.

"Do you want another drink?" Jordie points at my cup.

"No, thanks. It's still full."

"Cool. Be back in a bit." He pulls away.

Letting out a sigh of relief, I drop my head back.

"Riveting conversation," a deep voice says close behind my ear.

I turn. "Austin—"

Jeans, cowboy boots, and a button-down are just too dangerous a combination, especially when he's got that beard and those sparkling blue eyes.

"Wonder if he'll ask about urinals next," Austin says.

I giggle. "I hope not."

My eyes drift down to the cross necklace around his neck. It's tucked away but not hidden.

I look back up, offering him a bemused smile. "So… are you going to eavesdrop on my conversations all night?"

There's a cute smirk on his face. "I won't have to eavesdrop if you talk to me for the rest of the night."

"Wow… you have a big ego! Why have I never noticed that before?"

"I never used to have an ego…" He rubs the back of his curly blond head. "But then this girl I know kept kissin' me, and I thought maybe she knows somethin' I don't."

79

My cheeks flare with heat. I'm thankful we're outside and it's too dark for him to notice... I think.

"You like bringing that up, don't you?"

He grins. "There's no use in feelin' awkward about it. Besides, I've had a few drinks. I can't help myself."

My gaze drifts down to his can of beer. I notice his hand gripping the can. His nails are short, clean, and well-groomed. I blush and smile to myself as I think about Crystal's words from earlier.

"You got a tattoo?" He asks.

"Oh... yeah." I lift my arm so he can get a better view of the tattoo under my armpit, on my ribs. "I forget it's there sometimes. It's a golden shellback."

"A golden wha—?" He narrows his gaze. "Looks like a turtle to me."

"It *is* a turtle."

"Well, you shoulda said that the first time! There's no way I know what a golden seashell is."

I laugh. "A golden shellback. It's symbolic—it means I've traveled over the equator."

"Ah." He pulls back. "It's one of those tattoos you gotta earn."

"Exactly."

"I'm surprised it ain't a toilet."

I laugh, accidentally snorting in the process. I cover my mouth in embarrassment. He watches me as if it's endearing.

"Any other tattoos you're plannin' on earnin'?"

"Well... I'll get a swallow one day. It means returning home after an adventure."

He raises his brows. "A swallow?"

"It's a bird."

"Dang. You're on your way to havin' a whole damn zoo tattooed on your body!"

I laugh. "Well, I'm not getting a swallow any time soon. And neither are you, I'm sure. Are you planning on living in Seattle forever?"

"I'll come back eventually," he says. "Home ain't goin' anywhere."

Taking a sip from my big red cup, I stare at him unapologetically. Why does he have to be so incredibly handsome?

"Why are you talking to me?" I ask.

"What d'ya mean?"

"There are plenty of other women here... ones who will cook your meals and clean your socks."

He chuckles. "You think that's what I want?"

"Isn't it?"

"I can pay people to make me food and do my laundry."

"So…"

"I'm hangin' out with you because you laugh at my dumb jokes." His voice becomes more intimate. "And I don't know when I'll see you again, Graceless—I mean, Grace."

Looking down at my drink, I smile to myself. When I look back up, I see his sparkling blue eyes staring into mine.

"You're beautiful," he says.

My cheeks instantly start burning. He's doing a really good job of making me want to kiss him again.

The tall skinny toilet guy shows up again with two red cups. "I know you said you didn't want another drink but I got one for you anyway."

He places a red cup in my free hand.

"Oh." I'm now holding two drinks. "Thanks?"

81

Austin's jaw pulses. I can tell he doesn't appreciate having his romantic advances blocked by a man who can't grow a beard. Holding both drinks, I look around for Crystal and Brad, seeing if they'll take over supervision duties for their strange friend.

"What did I miss?" Jordie asks.

"Grace and I were talking," Austin says. There's a note of territorialism in his voice. "Maybe you should give us some space."

"Chillax, man! We're all here to have fun." Jordie puts his arm around me, grabbing my shoulder. His thumb rubs my skin suggestively, causing the strap of my top to slide off my shoulder.

"Oh—" Feeling exposed, I go to fix it but I can't. I'm holding drinks in both hands. Instead, I roll my shoulder away from Jordie but pulls me closer.

Austin steps closer. "Get the hell off her."

Jordie tightens his grip on my shoulder. "You don't speak for her!"

I try to pull away again. Before I know it, Austin is lunging for Jordie, pinning him to the ground.

"Apologize!" He demands.

"Austin!" I drop both drinks. Sticky bourbon lemonade splashes all over my feet and flip-flops. Lunging forward, I try to pull Austin off Jordie but he's too big. I can't make him budge, not even half an inch. As I pull back, I realize there's suddenly a lot of attention on us.

"Get off me!" Jordie tries to land a punch but Austin easily grabs his fist and holds it frozen in place.

"Apologize," Austin demands, pinning Jordie harder onto the ground.

The music is still playing but people are stopping to watch the commotion. A few other guys try to give Austin a hand.

82

He puts his hand out to stop them. "Don't. I have this under control. He'll apologize, and then he'll leave this party. Ain't that right?"

Jordie hesitantly nods before finally looking over at me. "Sorry."

Austin lets go and Jordie quickly crawls away, rubbing his wrists. Austin faces me. His face is pink and he's breathing heavily.

"What the hell, Austin?" I shake my head. "This isn't the hockey rink."

"I wasn't gonna let him touch you like that."

"It wasn't a fair fight! You were twice his size."

"And he was twice yours... you think it's fine for him to grab you like that?"

More people are stopping to watch us. As I look around at all the curious faces, I feel heat flare in my cheeks. Looking back at Austin, I swallow.

"Excuse me."

Pulling away, I rush through the grass and to the house with my sticky feet. People are in the living room playing poker and others are in the kitchen chatting and making drinks. Ignoring everyone, I make my way to the basement where I can be alone.

The basement is dark and empty. My eyes adjust to the darkness as I spot the couch and the TV. The bass from the music outside is pulsing through the walls. Taking time to breathe, I try to process everything as adrenaline floods through me.

"I am strong," I mutter to myself. *"I don't need him looking out for me."*

Austin's actions were barbaric and completely inappropriate. Sure, they weren't as inappropriate as Jordie's actions... that guy was a real scumbag. At least Austin was

83

protecting me, making sure I was okay. I relive the moment when he lunged forward and pinned Jordie to the ground. All those muscles protecting me… it's not something I'm used to. Men usually take from me, deceive me, use me. But maybe Crystal is right… maybe Austin is built differently.

Touching my neck, I feel somewhat annoyed that I'm attracted to the idea of him protecting me. It feels so stereotypical… so superficial. But the sense of safety that I feel isn't superficial at all.

"Are you okay?" Austin's deep voice asks. His dark silhouette is standing at the bottom of the basement stairs.

I exhale forcefully. "Why do you always treat me like a little girl?"

"I'm not treatin' you like a little girl," he says. "I'm treatin' you like a woman—a queen. I protect you just like I protect my friends, my family, my team."

As I get closer, I look into his fierce blue eyes. A loud noise upstairs distracts me. We can hear voices near the stairs. Grabbing Austin's shirt—which is damp from a full day of doing god-knows-what with Joe—I pull him into the empty laundry room. It's a tight room and he's taking up most of the space. There's only an inch of air between us.

"We clearly want different things," I say in a hushed voice.

He shakes his head. "I don't think we do."

"I'm not marrying you."

"I ain't askin' you to marry me."

"What, then?" I look up into those sparkling blue eyes.

Before I know what's happening, he's lifting me and sitting me on top of the dryer. We're eye-to-eye now. *Holy crap… what's happening?*

"I want you, Grace," he says. His hands find my waist. "And I ain't waitin' another six years."

84

My legs naturally push apart as his body finds the space in between. His face is only inches from mine. I'm surrounded by the scent of cowboy cologne as I feel the warmth of his breath on my lips.

"What are we doing?" I whisper.

"You said you could meet halfway. Maybe I can too."

"How?"

"Well… you're gonna say that you want me back. And then I'm gonna kiss you."

My body is pulsing with heat as my mind races. His lips are inches from mine, tempting me to find out how soft they are. He's looking at me in a way I've never been looked at before—like he'll destroy the world and everyone in it just to keep me safe. I've never felt this way before. Suddenly there's an emotional energy that I can't control. Looking into those blue eyes, I nod.

"I want you." My breath is barely louder than a breath.

Without wasting another second, he presses his lips against mine. It's on. Our lips mash together like a tornado meeting a hurricane. The intensity is furious and sudden. His busy lips taste like bourbon lemonade. Grabbing my waist, he pulls me harder against him. He's touching me with such confidence and conviction—he's definitely not treating me like a little girl anymore.

As the bass pulses outside, all I'm aware of is the sound of us trying to catch our breath as we devour each other. We connect in a way I never thought possible. We needed this.

A distant voice from the top of the stairs calls out. *"Austin!"*

Austin doesn't stop. I get the feeling that there's nothing in the world that could pull his attention off me. There's nothing more important right now. Everything is fast and hot. The air is humid as our lips continue exploring each other.

More voices call from the other room. Although I don't want to, I pull away.

"You should go," I say as I catch my breath. "It's your party."

A dissatisfied growl escapes his throat as he nibbles at my neck.

"I wanna stay here," he says.

Chills run up my spine as he holds my waist and continues to kiss my ear. I use my legs to invite him closer. He understands the assignment. Pressing his body harder against mine, he wraps his muscular arms securely around me. I close my eyes and lean my head to the side, allowing the sensation of his lips on my neck to flood through me. A deep primal groan rumbles in his throat as he kisses me.

My brother's voice calls out clearer this time. *"Austin!"*

That moan of pleasure vibrating in Austin's throat turns into a moan of annoyance. He pulls back and looks into my eyes. I can tell what he's thinking. *What now?*

"I'll find you later," he whispers. He pulls out of the laundry room and lets the door close behind him. "Hey, Joe. What's up?"

"Where've you been?"

Joe is right outside the laundry room. I stay seated on the dryer, hidden from sight. All I can hear is my racing heart and my heavy breathing. I hear their footsteps as they go up the stairs. Everything feels surreal. I feel like I need time to process what just happened. What happens now? I don't know. I'm too euphoric to think about that. My blood is pumping and my heart is racing. Taking a few minutes to catch my breath and fix my disheveled hair, I step out and head up to my room.

86

***

The party rages on into the early morning. I manage to sleep in a bit before waking up not long after sunrise. As I make my way downstairs, I notice that the house isn't as much of a mess as I expected it to be. The backyard, however, is littered with empty beer cans and streamers.

Although I barely even had one drink last night, I still feel like I have a hangover—an emotional hangover. I still can't believe that Austin and I kissed. *Finally.* I'm surprised he even kissed me after his speech the other night about wanting all of me. I knew he'd give in to the temptation.

I wonder if he's already on his way to the airport. My stomach drops as I wonder when I'll ever see him again. It could be in six weeks or six years.

My empty belly aches as I pull the fridge open. The great part about Joe being so successful is that he always keeps the fridge stocked. I find everything I could possibly want to eat while I'm hungover—eggs, bacon, and all the ingredients to make pancakes. Within half an hour, I've got a breakfast fit for a queen, including hot coffee to wash it all down.

As I sit at the dining room table and eat, I wonder what my next steps will be. Now that Austin is gone, I can focus on getting out of Tennessee. I'll have to look for a job and save enough money for a flight and a week's stay at a hostel.

Even just thinking about the hostel gives me unpleasant memories. I hate that my experience was ruined because of that douchebag.

I hear Joe yawn loudly as he enters the dining room. His shaggy hair is more of a mess than usual. He spots the breakfast on the table. "Yum!"

"You're up early," I say.

He shrugs. "This body only needs a few hours of sleep to function. Pass me that pot of coffee and I'll be functioning at full capacity."

I pass the pot of coffee over. As he fills his mug, he looks up at me.

"It's nice having you back, Gracie."

"Yeah…"

"You should come back for Christmas. You shoulda seen the lights I put up last year!"

"I saw the pictures."

"Pictures didn't do it justice."

If I come back for Christmas, I might see Austin. Would that be awkward? Or would we pick up right where we left off? There's a squeak as the basement door opens. A few seconds later, Austin appears in the doorway.

"Austin!" I nearly drop my fork. "I didn't know you were still here."

He runs his hand through his blond curls. We stare at each other for a moment.

"Mornin'," he says.

"You hungry?" Joe asks.

He touches his belly and stares at the empty spot at the head of the table, right next to me.

"I should really be gettin' goin'… I need to drive Ma to church. But I've got time for a bite or two."

"I'll get you a plate." Joe makes his way to the kitchen.

Austin takes his seat.

"Hey," he says. His eyes are on me.

"Hey." I swallow. "Did you have fun last night?"

"Sure did." There's a glint of mischief in those eyes. "Were you expectin' me to leave without sayin' goodbye?"

88

"No," I lie. I feign interest in the small pool of syrup on my plate.

He leans in, forcing me to look into his eyes. "Are you gonna come with me, or what?"

Wide-eyed, I look up at him. "Go with you? Go where?"

"To Seattle… I want you to travel with me."

The answer surprises me. "Travel with you?"

"Stay with me. When the team travels, you can come with us. You can stay at the hotel with me, go to games, explore the city, volunteer—do whatever you want. If you don't wanna be with me anymore, come back home. Do your own thing. And if you really don't wanna see me, you can hide from me for the rest of your life. But I'm still gonna be a part of this family whether you like it or not."

Stunned, I nod. "Okay… point taken."

"Good." He watches me. "So, that's a yes?"

"What makes you think I'm gonna cater to your plans so easily?"

"Because I know the way you feel about me," he says with a smirk as he leans in. "I saw that look in your eye last night."

I lift my chin. "What look?"

"Like you wanna have my babies."

Half in shock and half-amused, I look at the door to make sure Joe can't hear us. "Are you crazy?"

He smirks. "Probably."

Joe walks back into the dining room with a plate of eggs. Austin and I pull away from each other.

"Here you go." Joe places the plate on the table.

"Thanks."

Joe takes a seat. "Excited for the new hockey season?"

Austin nods as he pours hot sauce over the eggs. "It's bittersweet. I love gettin' back to hockey, but I hate leavin' Tennessee."

"It won't be long before you're back. I think the Blades play in Memphis in the fall. I'll be sitting in the front row!"

Anxious to get back to our conversation, I search for a way to get Joe to leave again. Spotting the cold and almost-empty pot of coffee, I see my solution. I reach for the pot of coffee, pretending that I'm about to pour Austin a cup.

"Oh no, it's empty," I say. "I'd make you more but I almost broke Joe's fancy coffee machine this morning trying to make the first pot."

Joe sighs. "Give me that."

He grabs the empty pot from me and heads to the kitchen. I'm not proud of my reverse psychology skills, but they do come in handy during moments like these. When he's out of earshot, I look back at Austin.

"You really want me to go to Seattle with you?"

He nods.

"Like… forever?"

He shrugs. "That's up to you."

I laugh. "You're fucking crazy."

"Travel with me for a few weeks," he says. "If you don't like spending that much time with me, come back. It's that easy."

"But I have to work, I have to save up money—"

"I'll take care of you," he says. "You'll always have a roof over your head and food on the table. I'll give you enough money to fund another one of your trips. You can volunteer as much as you want without worrying about anythin'."

"You would do that?"

"Yes, ma'am."

90

"Hmm…"

"What?"

"You expect me to leave again, meaning you don't think I'll be sticking around," I say.

"That ain't true. I believe in us. And all it takes is one believer to change everythin'."

I smirk as I look at him.

"I'm meetin' you halfway," he says. "Just like you wanna meet me halfway."

"Why?"

He keeps his unwavering gaze on me. "There's a lot of unfinished business between us, Grace. And I don't wanna live life without seein' what could happen."

His words stun me for a moment. I think about his proposition. Traveling across the US would be interesting. I could volunteer in different cities without worrying about making money. And I'll be able to spend time with Austin. I thought all I wanted to do was kiss him, but now I realize I want to spend time with him. This isn't what I expected. I thought we'd have a short whirlwind romance followed by another six years of not seeing him. But now he wants to be in close quarters with me. He wants to *live* with me. He'll see everything there is to see of me—my faults, my flaws, my vulnerabilities. It's a scary thought.

"You don't think we'll get sick of each other?" I ask.

He chuckles. "It's been six years… we might need a lifetime to catch up on everything we've missed."

I gnaw on my lower lip as I gaze mindlessly at my half-eaten pancakes.

"You promised you wouldn't break my heart," Austin says. I look into his blue eyes—the bluest eyes I've ever seen. "And last night, you said that I was yours."

"At that moment, I was."

"That's BS. You know what you meant."

I stay silent.

He leans in. His breath is warm on my lips. "I'm plannin' on keepin' you to your word, Grace Lawless."

He kisses me gently. Syrup glues our lips together for a microsecond before he pulls away.

"You're an evil man, Mr. Berr," I say softly.

"Maybe meeting halfway could be fun." Smirking at me, he pulls back.

"Leaving?" Joe walks into the room with a fresh pot of coffee.

"Yeah," Austin says. "I gotta get to church. Ma won't be happy if I miss it."

"Dang, alright. Let me know the next time you're in town."

"Yeah... I'll see you." He looks back at me. "Thanks for the breakfast."

"Don't mention it."

"Bye, Grace."

I swallow and nod. "Bye."

His gaze lingers before he finally backs away and leaves. The door shuts and suddenly the house feels silent.

"Well, I gotta check on the Memphis location." Joe knocks back his cup of coffee. "The cleaning people are coming over in about an hour. Just FYI."

I'm barely listening to Joe as I run scenarios through my head. It's crazy. How can we meet halfway when he told me he wants a future with me? How can anyone meet halfway from there? I sigh. Maybe I did a good job convincing him to do something casual. Maybe he's ready for a whirlwind romance. As I think about it, it doesn't seem possible. But who knows? Stranger things have happened.

After a quick shower, I use Joe's laptop to check my messages. I still haven't replaced my stolen cell phone. As I open my messages, I see a message from Austin.

AUSTIN: It's your choice

There's an attachment. I open it and see a plane ticket to Seattle scheduled for a week from now. Maybe he's serious about meeting halfway. I guess there's only one way to find out.

— 8 —

AUSTIN

Freshly resurfaced ice, new jerseys, and fresh laces—
it could only mean one thing: it's the start of a new
hockey season. The Blades are back on the ice. We've got a
few more practices before we hit the road. Like clockwork,
the temperature's gettin' cooler now that I'm back in Seattle.
I already miss the country roads and apple pie, but there's
nothing like the excitement and potential of a new hockey
season.

"The dream team's back together." I skate over to Logan
Drake, Harrison Cooper, and Konstantine Ivanov. I've been
playing with them on the first line for several years now.

"I missed you, boys," Logan says. He looks over at
Cooper whose long hair makes him look like a Viking
warrior. Logan pinches Cooper's cheek. "And I missed this
adorable face."

Cooper swats him away and rubs his cheek. "I literally
saw you yesterday."

"Yeah, but I still missed you," Logan says, seeming offended that Cooper doesn't miss him back. "Besides, Konstantine's cheek is too skinny for me to pinch."

The Russian left winger smirks. "I'll fatten up for you."

"Where's PJ?" I look around for fellow defenseman, PJ Rance. He's been the highest-scoring defenseman on our team for the past several years. He's standing on the other side of the rink. Johnny Breakwood glides over instead.

"Hello, boys," Breakwood says. The six-foot-four defenseman might be slightly taller than me, but at least I've got a better beard.

"You on our line?" I ask.

He nods. "On Coach's orders. I guess he wants to switch things up."

"Well, welcome to the first line," Logan says. "You'll be in good hands with Austin."

I nod. "Let's make this season count."

"Hell yeah, brother." He fist-bumps me.

We continue with our practice. I pour everything I have into each drill. All I want is to sync up with my teammates, making sure we move like liquid on the ice. Every summer, I forget how much I love hockey—the way I feel free, the way I push myself. If I ain't sweatin' by the end of the hour, I ain't tryin' hard enough.

At the end of the practice, I skate over to Cooper.

"Captain," I say.

"Yeah?" He takes off his helmet and flips back his hair which is drippin' sweat.

"What can I do to get better the ice?"

"To get better?"

"Yeah… how can I start scorin' more goals?"

"Erm." Cooper runs his hand through his damp hair. "Practice your stick handling. And make yourself more available around the net. Work on those two things and we'll go on from there."

I nod. "Thanks, Captain."

Rinsing off quickly in the showers, I catch up with Dean so that we can drive home together. Dean Oakley has been one of my best friends on the team. Last year, I moved into a new condo which happens to be right across from his. Being neighbors is fun. It's nice having someone familiar in the neighborhood. It also means we carpool a lot, and since I'm the only one with a car, he tends to pay for most of my gasoline bill. I ain't complainin'.

"What was that all about?" He's in the passenger seat eating from a big bag of beef jerky.

"Oh, nothin'. Just asking for advice on how to improve my skills this year."

"Improve your skills? Where'd that come from?"

I shrug. "Just somethin' Pa told me to do on my birthday. He's got a point. I'm not gonna be the big strong guy forever. I'm not even the biggest or strongest guy on my line."

"If you need someone to practice drills with, I'm your man."

"Thanks." I grip the steering wheel.

"You alright, man?"

"Yeah, why?"

"You're all tense looking."

"We just had practice."

He laughs. "Naw, that's not it. Usually, you're all cocky and confident at the beginning of the season, but you've been distracted."

I run my hand through my wet hair. "I've got a lot on my mind."

"It's a girl, isn't it?"

There's no point in denying it.

"A woman," I say. Grace ain't a girl. Not anymore.

"I *knew* it! What's wrong? She doesn't own a big enough pumpkin patch? She's not Ma-approved?"

"Heh. Naw, none of that. It's just... it's complicated. That's all you gotta know."

It's been a week and Grace still hasn't responded to my message. I don't expect her to. I expect her to keep me on my toes for as long as I know her. I figured if I gave her a week to think about it, she'd eventually come around. Besides, I know how uncomfortable she feels in Tennessee. She still has a lot of memories of her mom there. I know I can't blame her for wantin' to move on.

I check the time on the dashboard. It's nearly seven in the evening. Grace's flight was supposed to land a few hours ago. I thought I'd see her before I went to practice, but I haven't heard a thing from her. I have no way of knowing if she even got on the plane.

I've been here before. I know what it's like to be ghosted by Grace Lawless. But I'm holding on to my personal philosophy—PMA: positive mental attitude. I saw the way she looked at me that night in the basement. I know how she feels about me.

Stopping in front of Dean's building, I look over at him. "See you tomorrow?"

"Yeah, buddy." He climbs out of the car. "Hey! Take a bath or something. I can't stand seeing you so tense."

I chuckle. "You gonna tell me to use bubble bath and candles too?"

"Hey, if it helps, it helps! Who am I to judge?"

97

I smirk. "Thanks for the advice."

He closes the door. I pull down the block and into the underground parking of my building. Grabbing my gym bag, I take the elevator up to the sixteenth floor. As I step out onto my floor, I see a woman standing in the hallway in front of my door.

A slow smile transforms my face. "Well, well, well. If it ain't Grace Lawless on my doorstep."

As I walk up to her, I spot the overnight bag strapped over her shoulder. She's in a black pullover sweater and baggy army-green cargo pants.

"Look who decided to show up."

She smiles that smile that just melts me. "Surprised to see me?"

"Not really," I say.

She plays with the strap of her bag. "Well, you should know... I'm here for the travel. And the volunteer opportunities."

I smirk. "So, you're not here for me?"

She purses her lips and lifts her chin. "I'm meeting you halfway."

I nod. "Halfway. Okay."

Her hazel eyes watch me. I can tell that we both feel the electricity stormin' between us.

Looking around, she crosses her arms. "I'm surprised a professional hockey player doesn't have the floor to himself."

"Are ya disappointed?"

She laughs. "Definitely not! I've been living in hostels for the past few years. As long as you've got a bed and running water, I'll be more than satisfied."

I chuckle to myself. "I may be a millionaire, but I'm still just a humble boy from Tennessee."

"Clearly."

Our eyes connect and she smiles again. This is it. This is all I needed—a sign that she'd be willing to at least try. I can meet her halfway. I can meet her more than halfway. But I won't hesitate to push her to the edge and maybe even over it. I'll push her just enough so that she'll fall for me. And from what I'm feeling right now, that won't be very hard.

"Come on," I say. "Let me show you inside."

— 9 —

GRACE

Not sure if this is really happening, I follow Austin into his apartment. The lights automatically turn on as we step inside. I reluctantly place my travel bag on the floor by the door. I have *no* clue what I'm getting myself into. I'm not sure if I'm excited or if this is the worst fucking idea ever. On paper, everything about this seems perfect… I can travel to different cities, I can volunteer, *and* I can kiss Austin again. I've spent the last week thinking about him and that kiss. My god. Making out with Austin Berr exceeded all my expectations, yet I'm still not satisfied. I need more time with those lips.

On the other hand, so many things can go wrong. What if things are awkward if alcohol is not involved? I've always felt that the more elusive I am, the more interesting I am. Spending so much time with Austin could make him realize that I'm not as interesting as he thinks I am. I don't want to overstay my welcome. If this turns into a dumpster fire, I'll have many years of cringing ahead of me.

"This is my place," he says.

"It's nice." I barely notice the apartment. My eyes are fixated on Austin. He's in sweatpants and a black t-shirt. His hair is still damp and he smells like that delicious masculine scent he always exudes after a workout.

Before he can catch me staring at him, I look around the apartment. The architecture is modern with tall ceilings, track lighting, and a shared kitchen and living room space. The tall white walls are bare and there isn't very much decor. The furniture is simple and only there out of necessity—a big black couch, an unremarkable dining room table, and two stools by the kitchen island. The only personal items are a few medals hanging on the wall, some old DVDs by the big-screen TV, and some framed pictures. Austin clearly doesn't have a designer's touch, but the simplicity of it all is kind of endearing.

Looking back, I see him with his hands in the pockets of his sweatpants. He's lifting his chin, looking confident and cocky. He smirks.

"What?" I ask.

He shakes his head. "Nothin'. I just never expected to see Grace Lawless standing in my living room."

My gaze flashes down to the floor as I shyly push my dark hair behind my ear. I'm not usually shy. I usually take the lead when it comes to sexual advances, but with the way he's looking at me, it's clear that Austin has all the power. The man's got lust in his eyes.

Resisting him a bit, I decide to go slow. I told him I'd meet him halfway, and that's what I'm gonna do. I continue looking around the apartment. I see a few framed pictures. Some are of him and his family, others are of him with friends.

My eyes widen. "What's this?"

101

I grab the frame and look closer. It's a picture of Austin and Joe. In the background, there's me photobombing them. I'm tilting my head to the side and making a funny face.

"Oh." He chuckles as he scratches the back of his head. "That's a picture of us at the monster truck rally. Remember that?"

Staring at the photo, I nod. "Yeah. You waited in line for over twenty minutes to buy a bag of caramel corn only to spill it the moment you got to your seat."

He laughs. "That's right."

"The look on your face was so sad. It still breaks my heart when I think about it." Scanning the rest of the photos, I notice one of Austin standing with what looks like a child in a hospital gown. "Who's this?"

Austin looks at the photo. "Oh, that's Jimmy. I met him at the children's hospital a few years back. I go there every once in a while to spend the day with the kids."

"Wow. I didn't know you did that."

"I don't do it as much as I should… I've made a lot of little friends at that hospital. Lost a few too." He looks down at the picture. "Jimmy was one of them."

I look at the little boy and his haunting smile. "He looks like he went through a lot."

"Yeah… I miss the little guy."

Watching Austin, I realize that he's a mature version of the young man I used to know. After all, he was just a teenager when I first knew him. He's obviously grown a lot since then. And even though I've met many male volunteers during my travels, Austin seems to have more compassion in his eyes than all of them put together. It's a side of him I didn't know existed. It's… attractive.

He catches me staring at him. A slow smile plays on his lips. "I like the way you look at me."

The sexual tension hums between us. The temperature in my body raises. I clear my throat.

"I like the simplicity of this place." I change the topic, hoping to diffuse the tension in the room.

"It's bare, that's for sure. I ain't the best decorator." He chuckles as he scratches the back of his blond curls. "I could definitely use some help."

I laugh. "Well, don't ask me. My decorating skills only appeal to people who like glow-in-the-dark stars on their ceiling."

He rubs his short scruffy beard as he looks up. "Those could look good here."

His silly comment makes me laugh. "I don't think you have a ladder that tall."

"Oh, trust me. I could find one."

I smirk. Looking down, I get lost in my thoughts for a moment.

"It's weird," I say. "I haven't had a room to call my own since high school. With all the traveling, I've never settled anywhere."

"I know the feelin'. I'm always travelin' too… I'm either on the road with the team or back home in Tennessee."

"At least you have this place."

"You've got your old room," he says.

"That's true… but it's different now. My mom's not around anymore and Joe owns the house… that room doesn't feel like mine anymore. It's like it's from a different era… it's hard to explain."

Furrowing his brow, he watches me with a contemplative expression. "Do you ever think you'll stop travelin' and settle down?"

I hesitate. "I don't know… maybe. After what happened a few weeks ago, it seems more likely."

"Why?"

My heart is racing at the mere thought of the robbery and my night sleeping out on the street.

"It seems like a silly thing to be scared about," I say.

"No. It's not silly at all. Someone took advantage of you. It was a traumatic event."

I let out a big breath. "I took so many risks going out there, being on my own… I can't help but feel like I was punished for making those choices."

"Are you kiddin'? You're gonna let one asshole ruin everything for you? Bad things happen. That's life. You can't let it stop you."

"Yeah…" I look into his eyes. My heart rate is finally slowing down.

"But if you're seriously done sleepin' in hostels, I'll admit that havin' a place of your own is pretty nice too. I mean, know this place is pretty empty and I'm never here, but it's my own little kingdom."

I look around. "This doesn't seem like a kingdom fit for Austin Berr."

"Oh yeah?" Bemused, he raises his brows. "What kind of kingdom should I have?"

"Hmm… I don't think you're meant for the city. You should have a nice house out in the country on a big farm somewhere. Maybe somewhere cold where you could flood your backyard and make a skating rink."

He chuckles. "You've been thinkin' hard about this."

"Not really. I just get that vibe from you."

"Or maybe I can have a farm near the ocean. That way we can go swimmin'."

I raise my brows. "We?"

He steps closer. "We're meetin' halfway, right?"

"Right."

"What's that mean?" He looks at me in a way I've never been looked at before.

Heat floods my cheeks. "Well... I won't treat us like a one-night-stand, and you won't write me into your will."

He chuckles. His voice becomes deep and intimate. "And where exactly does that leave us?"

"I'm not sure... I guess it means we're getting to know each other."

"Alright." He straightens his posture. "What do you want to know about me?"

"Umm..." I bite my lip as I think. When I can't think of anything, I laugh. "I don't know."

"Maybe we know each other too well."

I purse my lips. "Okay, then... boxers or briefs?"

A mischievous smile appears on his face. "Do you want me to tell you? Or do you wanna find out for yourself?"

I've lost track of how many times Austin has made me blush so far tonight. I'm grinning so wide that I'd give the Cheshire Cat a run for his money.

"Well... what do you know about me?" I lift my chin and look into his eyes as I challenge him. "If you know me so well, enlighten me."

"You're stubborn and fearless. You're smart but you still laugh at my dumb jokes. You don't care about money or status. And you're an atheist—sorry, agnos—" He furrows his brow.

"Agnostic," I say.

"That's it. You're agnostic, but you're more altruistic than anyone I've ever met."

My lips part slightly. He steps closer.

"And you think there's value in bein' mysterious, but you also crave intimacy." Noticing my reaction, he smirks slightly. "Am I wrong?"

Half-stunned and half-amused, I shake my head. "You think I crave intimacy?"

"You're here right now, aren't ya?"

I don't say anything.

"So, Grace…" His voice drops to a dangerous level. "Tell me something I don't know about you."

I confidently look up into his blue eyes. My mind races as I think about all the secrets I could tell him.

"You don't know what I'm like in bed."

There's a slight smirk on his lips. "Are you suggesting we change that? Because we can go do that right now."

Talking about it is only turning me on more. I assume he can see the lust in my eyes because I see the same look in his eyes. Stepping closer, he leans in and kisses me. Softly at first as if seeking approval. There's no way I'd deny him. I bury my fingers in his damp curls, pulling him closer. The passion between us is just as strong as it was at the party. No alcohol required.

There's no cowboy cologne tonight—just the scent of shampoo, fresh laundry, and raw masculinity. His natural odor brings me back to my high school days. As his mouth slides over mine, his hands find my lower back, gently pulling at my sweater and grazing my exposed skin with his fingertips. A chill runs up my spine. I pull my lips from his.

"Is that halfway?" His lips are red and full.

My head is spinning. I'm overwhelmed by the combination of his masculine scent, the firm tone of his voice, and that arousing kiss. I know I wanted to resist him for as long as possible but I'm only human. Grabbing his

106

shirt, I pull him against me and we enthusiastically pick up where we left off. His mouth slides over mine. His hands are on my back again as his skin makes contact with mine. He's touching me on his terms and I'm letting him do whatever he wants.

"I thought you didn't want this," I say. My voice is barely a whisper.

"Oh, I definitely want this." His lips are on my neck, traveling up to my earlobe. "I said I didn't want a one-night stand."

He pulls back and looks into my eyes.

"You're not leavin' tomorrow, are you?" He asks.

My lips are still buzzing. I shake my head.

"Good," he says.

I put my hand on his chest. "But I thought you were a good church-going boy."

He smirks. His sinfully sexy eyes sparkle. "You said I wasn't one."

"Good point."

His grip on my waist loosens. "We don't have to do this… I mean, I *really* want to. But we don't have to if you don't want to…"

I shake my head. "Fuck that."

Grabbing his shirt, I pull him close, kissing him again. Without missing a beat, he lifts me and wraps my legs around his waist. He balances me on the back of the couch as his mouth does magical things to mine. Twisting my long hair out of the way, he nibbles on my neck. Dropping my head back, I moan.

"It's so hot," I whisper.

"I can take care of that." His large hands grab at my sweater and easily pull it off, exposing my bra. He tosses the sweater aside and goes back to kissing the sensitive area over my collarbone. His beard tickles my sensitive skin as he moves down to my breasts, kissing me through the sheer black fabric of my bra. As his kiss turns ravenous, the peaks of my nipples harden and a fullness throbs between my legs. I instinctively grind against him to find some relief. The hard bulge under his sweatpants tells me he's getting just as aroused as I am. I arch my back and grind needily against him. He holds me against him as his lips find my ear.

"Slow down." His voice is so deep that I feel it in my bones.

"I can't help it when you're torturing me like this."

He laughs. "Torture? I thought that was pleasure."

I stretch, still trying to press against him. "You're going so slow."

"It's payback for makin' me wait a week to see if you were comin' or not." He keeps kissing me. "I want you to feel the slow agony that I felt."

There's that competitive male energy that I remember from when he was a teenager.

"Slow agony?" I ask. "Was waiting a week really that bad?"

He smirks. "You think pleasure's torture, so... I don't think you're allowed to judge me. Now, hold still so that I can unhook your bra and continue torturin' you."

I straighten my back. I'm not moving anymore, but I can feel that he's more aroused now. As his warm hands move up my back, I'm tempted to move.

"Your bossiness is annoying," I say.

He chuckles. "You're gonna love it in a few minutes."

Unhooking my bra easily, he tosses it aside.

"Come." He easily lifts me and walks around the couch where he lays me down on it. He presses a button somewhere and the curtains start to automatically close.

Austin hovers over me as he dips his head down. He teases my nipples with his tongue, eventually making his way down my belly. He starts unbuttoning my pants. Throbbing with heat, I sit up and look at him.

"Am I the only one taking my clothes off tonight?"

I'm not ready for him to see just how damp with desire I am.

He smirks. Reaching over his head, he pulls off his t-shirt, revealing his defined body. He's got the perfect amount of body hair and abs that can't be bought. Not to mention the Tennessee tan. It does his body justice.

"That better?" He asks.

I hold my hands over my breasts and shake my head. "I want you to take it *all* off."

A shy smile appears on his face before quickly transforming into a confident one. "I thought I was calling the shots here."

"We're meeting halfway, aren't we?"

His sexy grin widens. "Alright."

Standing confidently, he pulls off the sweatpants. I get my answer to the boxers or briefs question: he wears neither. He simply springs out at full attention. Looking up into his eyes, I relax back onto the couch as I remove my hands from my breasts.

"Alright, then."

He pulls off my pants and everything else.

"I don't want anything between us," he says. Sitting on the couch, he pulls me on top of him. I'm momentarily shocked by our intimate skin-to-skin contact. He nuzzles my neck. "I wanna taste you."

His mouth explores mine. His hands move down my waist to my backside, fondling me hungrily.

"Austin-" I close my eyes and press my forehead against his. "Before we do this…"

We breathe heavily, our bodies rising and falling together.

Swallowing, I pull back and look into his eyes. "I… I…"

He pushes a strand of my hair off my face. I'm lost in his impossibly blue eyes.

"I know," he says.

Guiding my face, he kisses me again. The passion comes on suddenly. His tongue mimics the same thing he's doing between my legs—exploring, pressing, taunting. He arouses me to the point of insanity—until my body aches and my back arches, protesting the lack of deeper touch.

"I want you so badly," I whisper.

As if rewarding me for my confession, he gives me what I want. I gasp as we connect. I drop my head back as he holds me close, dragging his lips along my earlobe.

"You feel so good," he whispers. "I knew you'd be able to handle me."

His hands are still on my backside, guiding me along with his rhythm. The way he moves is violent and soft all at once. I hold on, connecting with him in a way I didn't feel possible. Sex has never felt like this before.

My body shakes as I feel the beginning of an orgasm I'm not sure I can handle. Austin feels it too. His fingers dig deeper into my thighs as I let out an involuntary moan.

My head is swimming and my body's tingling. We're in each other's arms, tired and out of breath. We're sweaty too. When did that happen?

110

Austin rests his head back against the couch and closes his eyes. "Whew. You take a lot out of me, Grace Lawless."

"If you want to rest, I can go clean up—"

"Are ya kiddin'?" He pulls me against him. Our sweaty bodies mash together. "I want you right here."

"Even though we're wet and sweaty?"

"*Especially* because we're wet and sweaty."

"Oh…" I graze his chest.

"And I wanna get you to make that noise again," he says. His hands are on my ass again, pulling me tighter against him.

"What noise?"

"The howl."

I laugh. "I didn't howl!"

"I definitely made you howl, and I'll do it again."

"No, I won't."

"Wanna bet?" He grins deviously as he begins kissing me.

***

Waking up the next morning, I find myself in Austin's bed, snuggled up against him. My arm is draped around his chest, rising and falling as he breathes. My eyes spring open.

Damn. Even when I'm unconscious, I can't resist putting my hands all over him. But I can't help it. I like the way I feel when I'm near him. I feel warm and protected.

I'm not used to this. I don't normally sleep over with guys after having sex. Beds in hostels aren't usually made for two. And the rooms in hostels usually have two or three other roommates sleeping a few feet away. Although romantic sleepovers happen—they're usually discouraged. And unwanted, by me.

111

Unsure what the protocol is for cuddling someone while they're sleeping, I roll back over to my side of the bed. A few seconds later, Austin rolls out of bed. Giving him a minute or two, I wait before rolling out of bed and pulling on a baggy shirt and some silky pajama shorts. I smell coffee so I assume Austin is in the kitchen. Rubbing my eyes, I make my way to the bathroom. Stepping inside, I quickly realize that Austin's not in the kitchen. The bathroom is full of steam and his naked body is barely obscured by the glass door. I see everything I didn't get to see last night. Water drips down his body as the water pours over his head. He shakes out his wet curls before turning around. Pulling away, I make my way to the kitchen. My cheeks flare with heat.

Why does he make me feel this way? I've seen guys naked before. Although, I've never seen guys look like *that*.

First, I woke up cuddling him… and now this? Feeling like the most awkward person alive, I go to the kitchen where fresh coffee is brewing in the pot. I hear the shower turn off in the other room. Grabbing a Blades mug out of the cupboard, I fix myself a cup of coffee just to appear busy.

Austin walks down the hall and into the kitchen. He's wearing a clean blue t-shirt that matches his eyes and comfy-looking black sweatpants. His hair is still damp from the shower. He walks over. His clean scent overwhelms the scent of fresh-brewed coffee.

"Good mornin'," he says.

"Morning." I lift the coffee mug to my lips.

"How'd you sleep?"

"Fine." I clear my throat. "Sorry for cuddling you this morning. I don't usually do that."

He chuckles. "Cuddle me whenever you want. The middle of the bed is halfway, ain't it?"

I smirk. "You're clever."

112

Grabbing a mug, he pours himself a coffee. "You're the only person who'll ever call me clever."

"Maybe I bring it out of you."

"Or you're the only person who sees it." He turns to me and takes a sip of black coffee. He leans back against the counter and watches me. "What are you gonna do today?"

"I don't know yet… why?"

He shrugs one shoulder. "You don't have a phone. I figure I should at least know *somethin'* about what you're doin'."

"To keep tabs on me?"

He chuckles. "Just in case somethin' goes wrong. Although, I can tell you wanna keep your secrets."

"It's fine… I'll tell you. I think I'll explore the city a little bit… scope out churches or shelters to volunteer at."

He nods. "I've got practice. But we should have dinner together."

"Like, make it together? We can do groceries together if you want."

He chuckles. "I meant like at a restaurant."

"Oh…"

"But if you wanna make dinner, we can do that too."

"You're in control, right? I'll do whatever you choose."

He smirks. I think we both know that neither of us has the control we think we do.

"The hockey schedule's in the printer. Check it out and see if any cities interest you."

"Oh… yeah." I forgot about this part of the plan. He wants me to satisfy my travel bug by following him around the country and staying with him at different hotels.

"We've got a game in San Francisco tomorrow, followed by one in Vegas. Pick where you wanna go, and I'll make sure to send you the plane tickets."

"Is this what life with you is gonna be like? A constant stream of plane tickets?"

He grins. "I thought you liked travelin'."

"And if I want to stay here in Seattle?"

"Do what you want, I can't stop you." A mischievous smile plays on his lips as he gets closer. His hands find my waist. "But I'd be *much* more satisfied if you came with me."

"So, that you can do this?" I ask, noting how handsy he's being.

"So that you can cuddle me when you're half asleep," he says.

I stiffen under his touch. My cheeks flare with heat.

"I was cold," I lie.

He smirks.

"I ain't judgin'. By the way..." His voice gets lower. "Next time you see me in the shower, feel free to join me."

My heart flutters and I suppress a smile. "Noted."

His eyes linger before he leans in to kiss me. I pull back, placing my hand over my mouth. He furrows his brow.

"I'm drinking coffee," I say.

"So?"

"My breath—"

He laughs. "Who cares? So do I. Come here."

He pulls me in and presses his soft lips against mine. Giving in, I relax under his touch and kiss him back. Every kiss with him is more incredible than the last. When he breaks the kiss, I grab his shirt to keep him close.

"Already?"

He smiles against my lips. "I've gotta get to practice. Dean's waitin' for me downstairs. I'll be back later, Graceless. Err—I mean, Grace."

"Can I confess something?"

"Yes, ma'am."

"I kind of miss hearing you call me Graceless."

His lips curl into a smile. "Well, then. I might have to fix that then."

I kiss him again.

"I gotta go." His lips graze mine. "I'll see ya later, Graceless."

My body is pounding with anticipation as he pulls away. Grabbing his gym bag, he leaves me alone with the sound of the gurgling coffee machine. With a goofy smile still plastered on my face, I check out the team schedule that he left for me. San Francisco, Vegas, Houston, New Orleans— this could be interesting. Setting the paper aside, I sip my coffee as I walk around the apartment. This is where I'll be living temporarily… or maybe even indefinitely. If this is what a future with Austin could look like, then this could be fun.

— 10 —

AUSTIN

Feeling like a king, I go into our first game day with confidence and bravado. Even the other guys notice it during our afternoon skate before our game in San Francisco.

I'm not sure I ever figured out where halfway is with Grace, but I'm enjoying it so far. She doesn't own much stuff, so there ain't much evidence that she's living with me, but if I squint I can see the signs. Her ballet flats are always by the door. I find half-full bags of potato chips around the house. My bed sheets always smell like her. Her black travel bag is always sitting in the corner of my room and her toothbrush is in my bathroom. It's right next to the case for my fake teeth. She's not disgusted about my teeth at all... hell, I think she even prefers me without 'em.

After the practice, I make my way to the inn by the bay. I'm not staying with the team at a hotel like I usually do. If this is my first night away with Grace, I want it to have a touch of romance. I don't think she's used to romance and

I don't think she even knows if she likes it. But I'll make sure to change that.

Entering the room at the inn, I look around. The room has dark blue walls and brass-colored nautical embellishments. The large windows look out onto the deep blue water only a few feet away. It feels like the room is in the water.

I look around for signs of Grace. The only sign I would find is her overnight bag, which I don't see. I sniff the air for her scent, but all I smell is the salty ocean and fresh towels. My mind races but I keep a positive mental attitude.

Everything's fine, I tell myself. She'll show up.

Ordering room service, I get a steak delivered to my room. I sit at the tiny desk in the corner of the room and eat while I check my messages. For what? Grace still doesn't have a phone. I insisted on buying her one but she said she liked the freedom of being unconnected. That's classic Graceless. She's like smoke—the more I try to grab at her, the more elusive she becomes.

But that's the price I pay to be Grace Lawless' man. It's all worth it to have her in my arms as we have our late-night conversations about Martians, God, and life. And the sex... the sex is incredible. It doesn't take long for our conversations to turn into flirty glances and heavy touching. Before I know it, she's sittin' in my lap and I'm pulling off her clothes. It's that easy with her. Things get so passionate that precautions are an afterthought. It doesn't matter. I'll take care of her no matter what happens.

After I finish eating my pre-game meal, I take a quick shower and put on a clean suit. Even though I'm trying to focus on hockey, everything brings my mind back to Grace. The scent of the lemongrass soap in the bathroom smells like her. The velvet cushions on the bed remind me of the

117

velvet top she was wearing when I kissed her on my birthday. And the scent of the salty ocean will always remind me of her the most.

Checking the time, I see that Grace should be here in the next half hour. I won't be around to see her until after the game. Grabbing the phone, I call the front desk.

"Alina speaking," a woman's voice says. *"How can I help you?"*

"Alina? Hi. I'd like to order some chocolate-dipped strawberries for the room. You can just bring them in and leave them on the desk."

"Yes, sir. Is that all?"

I think for a moment. "Can you bring up a couple bags of potato chips too?"

"Yes, sir."

"Thanks, Alina." After hanging up, I place the ticket for tonight's game on the desk. Using the room's notepad, I write a note.

Grace—
I got you some game snacks.
—Austin

Propping the note up on the desk, I make sure it's visible enough. When the strawberries and chips arrive, Grace will be sure to see the message.

An hour later, I'm in the arena. Energy is high for the first game of the season. The team floods out onto the ice for the pre-game warmup. Music pumps through the loudspeakers as fans begin to fill the stands. Skates scrape against the ice as we warm up. Looking out into the crowd, I find the spot behind the penalty box where Grace should be sitting. I don't see her yet.

Someone pushes me from behind. I turn to see Dean standing behind me.

"You no longer want to share a hotel room with me?" He asks. "What the hell! Do I stink or something?"

I laugh. "Sorry, man. Was I supposed to give you a formal warnin'?"

I watch as the rest of the guys take turns lobbing pucks at our goalie, Skip.

"It's your new girlfriend, isn't it?" Dean watches me.

"What?" I look at him. "How'd you know?"

"I can see *right* through your living room window, dude."

"You're watchin' us? What are you, some kind of pervert?" I laugh. "Are you filmin' us too?"

"Dude… you two were full-on making out the other night. It's hard not to notice a makeout session *that* intense." He's got a playful grin on his face.

Chuckling, I look up at the seat again. It's still empty.

Where is she?

Two guys skate toward us as they chase the puck, bumping into each other. It's Logan and Cooper.

"You're supposed to make me look good, Coop!" Logan chirps at him.

"Fine. Let's try again," Coop says. He takes control of the puck again. "Backhand or forehand? Between the legs or behind the back?"

Logan taps him playfully with his stick before they take off again.

I look back at Dean and shrug. "What can I say? I guess things are going pretty well."

119

"My man! That's what I like to hear." He playfully pushes me. "So, that means you're ready for today's game?"

Shaking my head, I look up at the stands again. *There she is.* Her long dark hair is draped over a purple jean jacket. My eyes connect with hers. I can see her gorgeous smile all the way from here. My shoulders relax. That's my girl. And I'm never lettin' her go.

"Austin?" Dean asks, shaking me back to reality.

Adrenaline pushes through my veins.

Smiling, I nod. "*Now*, I'm ready."

— 11 —

GRACE

Sitting in my seat in the San Francisco arena, I watch as the guys get ready for the puck to drop. The chilly air and the loud music energize me. Tapping my feet, I'm barely able to sit still in my seat.

The last time I watched Austin play hockey was back in high school. Sure, I watched him on TV once or twice a year—whenever I had internet access and our time zones lined up. But watching in person is a whole different experience. And this arena is a step up from the tiny one in high school.

I'm holding a bag of chips, and I've got a bag of caramel corn stashed away in my purse for Austin. I figured I should pick up some snacks for him since he left some for me in the room. I still have the taste of strawberries and chocolate on my lips.

He's too nice. Maybe even perfect. It's a bit mindblowing that he hasn't grown bored of me yet. A guy's never been interested in me for this long—or at least, I haven't given anyone the chance. And now I'm here with a man who's flying me across the country and buying me chocolate-covered strawberries. And it's not even the money or the gifts that I care about… I could live without them. It's his goofy personality and the way he lights up when he sees me. It's the way he can switch from flirtatious to controlling by slightly changing the tone of his masculine voice. And—it seems silly—but it's the way he cares about me. I don't feel trapped. That's not to say I don't feel how much he wants to possess everything about me—but I'm free to disappear without him breathing down my throat. He's shattering all my expectations of what I thought a man can be.

For the past week, I've been discovering Seattle. It's only been a week, but I've explored the neighborhood and found a women's shelter and a local church to volunteer at. I've also been getting used to Austin's apartment. It's a step up from a hostel, that's for sure. The bed is an upgrade too and so is the man that I share it with. Last night was the first night I had to sleep without Austin around and I actually missed him. It's crazy… it's only been a week and I *miss* him.

"Excuse me," a voice says. A man with a tray of nachos shuffles past me and sits in the vacant seat next to mine. "Hey."

I smile politely at him. "Hey."

"Huge fan."

I'm not sure if it's a declaration or a question. I give him a nod and pop some more chips in my mouth before I have to answer another non-question.

The game finally starts and the tension in the arena intensifies. Everyone gets quiet and moves to the edge of their seats as they watch the action. Grinning, I watch as Austin hops over the boards and gets into the play. There he is—strong, menacing, attractive. I can't stop staring at him.

He's focused and calculated, anticipating every move from the other players.

The San Francisco Whips take the early lead with a quick goal in the first five minutes but the Blades answer back a few minutes later. I quickly draw the ire of the surrounding fans as I cheer for the opposing team.

As the game continues, I become more and more invested. Halfway through the second period, the play is paused for a commercial break. The guys gather around the bench as the coach gives them instructions. Meanwhile, the arena announcer's voice is blasting over the loudspeakers.

"Now, if everyone looks up at the jumbotron, you'll see the kiss cam!"

I look up to watch on the big screen. The couple onscreen smiles in delight before kissing each other. The crowd cheers. A second couple is shown and the same thing happens. Amused, I watch with a smile. It's been so long since I've attended something like this. I've been to a few soccer games overseas, but this is an entirely different experience. As I watch the screen, I see dark hair and a familiar purple jacket.

Hey, I think to myself. *That looks like me.*

Then it hits me: That *is* me. The jumbotron is focused on me and the nacho man sitting next to me. He's looking at me with a wide grin on his face. I realize that everyone in our section is looking at us.

"I guess we gotta kiss now," he says.

Heat travels up the back of my neck and prickles around to my ears and face. He leans in, bringing his processed nacho cheese breath with him.

"I don't think so," I say.

The crowd laughs as I pull back but he grabs my wrist, pulling me closer. "The crowd wants us to!"

123

"Wait, no—"

He doesn't seem to be stopping. Determined to kiss me, he uses his iron grip to pull me even closer as he leans in with puckered lips.

I use my free hand to push him away as I avoid him. "Get off me!"

Before I have a chance to feel his nacho cheese lips on mine, I hear gasps in the crowd followed by an angry voice.

"Get off her!" An angry male voice says.

I open my eyes to see Austin climbing over the glass partition. Despite wearing ice skates, he manages to climb the concrete stairs easily as he rips his way over to us. Reaching over, he grabs the nacho man and easily pulls him out of his seat, pinning him to the stairs.

"What the *fuck* do you think you're doing?" Austin asks. "Is that how you treat women?"

"Oh my god!" I cover my mouth. A commotion erupts around me as people stand up, trying to see what's going on. I look up to see that the kiss cam is already focused on a different couple in an effort to divert attention away. It's not working. Everyone is watching and pulling out their phones.

Austin has tunnel vision and wants only one thing—to punish the nacho man. He holds the man tightly with his fists, lifting him a few inches off the ground and breathing heavily in his face. Austin's chest is rising and falling. He's not here to play. Feeling both horrified and fascinated, I watch.

The man looks at Austin with wide fearful eyes. "I should sue you!"

Austin laughs as he tightens his grip. "Sue me? My girlfriend will sue you for sexual harassment—it's all on film. And you'll be broke before you get the chance."

His girlfriend?

Security run down the stairs, prying Austin off the traumatized man. It takes three security guards to finally pull Austin away as they guide him up the stairs and away from the crowd. He looks back at me and I see those blue eyes. Adrenaline pounds through my veins. *Oh my god.*

Arena attendants guide the nacho man up the stairs and somewhere private. Meanwhile, I'm left with everyone's eyes on me. Even the players and referees on the ice are looking in my direction, wondering what the hell just happened. My throat is dry and my palms are sweaty. Making a decision, I follow the others up the stairs and away from the crowd.

Did that just happen? Did Austin just fight someone for me… again?

As I make my way to the hall where the beer vendors are, I take a moment to catch my breath and organize my thoughts. Not sure if I should stay or leave, I look around for guidance. One of the arena attendants approaches me. His nametag says his name is Bo.

"Excuse me, are you Grace Lawless?" He asks.

"Yes?"

"Mr. Berr has requested to see you."

"Okay…"

"Follow me."

Bo leads me down the hallway, through a restricted access door, and down a set of stairs.

"The visitor's locker room is right through this door," he says.

I look at the door and swallow. "Am I supposed to just go in?"

Waiting for Bo's answer, I look back to see that he's already gone. I hesitantly walk down the hallway which smells like sweat and testosterone. I haven't smelled anything

125

so strong since walking past the high school football team after gym class.

As I get closer to the visitor's locker room, I can hear two voices arguing.

"You're lucky that man didn't press charges!" An older man's voice says.

"He's lucky I didn't rearrange his face." Austin's voice is full of adrenaline and anger.

My heart is racing in my chest. Only Austin would express that much anger over another man disrespecting me.

"Twenty seconds and you need to get back on that bench," the older man says.

"Not until I see Grace."

I instinctively hold my breath so that I can hear better.

"Are you fucking kidding me?"

"No," Austin says in a dangerous tone. "She's more important to me than hockey."

Heart thumping in my throat, I step into the locker room. I can taste the sweat in the back of my throat. The sight of Austin distracts me from the odor. He's standing with the coach. I gently clear my throat and make myself known. They both look at me. Ignoring Coach, Austin rushes across the room to meet me.

"Grace…" His blue eyes search mine. The side of his eye is swollen. Drops of sweat are streaming down his face. "Are you okay?"

I look at him with a mix of horror and concern. "Austin… what the fuck?"

"He didn't hurt you, did he?"

"No… are you crazy?"

"I wasn't gonna let him kiss you like that."

126

I lower my voice. "I told you before… I don't need your protection."

He exhales heavily, clearly frustrated with me. "You might not need it but you're gettin' it anyway."

I don't know if it's the intensity of his voice, the smell of testosterone, or the adrenaline pumping through my blood—but everything about Austin is driving me wild right now. I'm annoyed that I'm attracted to such a brute, overprotective man.

"Your possessiveness is really something," I say.

"I ain't possessive, I'm protective."

"Well… are you sure you can control yourself?"

"I'm not out of control," he says. He reaches for me, grabbing my jean jacket and pulling me close against his warm, damp jersey. His hands grab needily at me as his voice lowers. "I told you I'd keep you safe, and that's what I'm doin'."

I can feel his breath on my lips as he looks into my eyes. *Oh wow.* He's told me these words before, but this time I believe it. I'm feeling emotions I've never felt before.

"Berr!" The coach barks from across the room.

Austin doesn't flinch. He keeps his intense blue eyes on me. He could give a fuck about the hockey game. All he cares about is me.

"You should go," I say.

He grabs needily at me again. "Tell me you're okay."

My eyes fix on his before I finally nod. "I'm fine."

"I'll see you at the inn." He watches me until I nod.

I take a step back. He holds onto my jacket, unwilling to let go until I finally pull away. "Get back out there, cowboy."

A slight smirk appears on his lips. "Yes, ma'am."

127

He looks at me one last time as if reassuring himself that I'm okay before pulling away. He walks across the locker room and leaves out the other end. The coach looks up at me with a weary glance before pulling away behind him. Feeling like I've overstayed my welcome, I leave.

Feeling a flurry of feelings, I'm too distracted to focus on hockey. Needing time to organize my thoughts, I head away from the arena and back to the inn.

***

I watch the rest of the game on the TV in our room at the inn. My mind is spinning. So much has happened in such a short time, it's hard to make sense of it all. I feel like I've realized something—or maybe I've known it all along—but I'm finally admitting it to myself.

The game ends with a win for the Blades. I turn off the TV and stare out at the violent water. The moon is shining over the dark ocean as waves crash onto the shore in a chaotic pattern.

Getting up, I walk outside. I'm in a tank top and my elephant pants, no shoes. My feet sink into the sand as I walk straight into the water. My clothes cling to my body as the violent waves crash around me. The ocean is the only thing that can wash away the chaos. Staring up at the stars, I disappear under the water. The whooshing sound of the ocean fills my ears.

I feel like two sides of me are fighting—my rational side and my emotional side. I've fought so hard against being an emotional person. But Austin is changing me.

Breaking through the surface of the water, I stand as my wet hair hangs heavy around my shoulders. Water drips down my face as I open my eyes. I see Austin standing at the

128

shore ten feet away. Waves are crashing at his feet. Although it's dark, there's still enough moonlight for me to see his face. He holds my gaze as he walks into the ocean to join me.

"You okay?" He asks. I feel his heat as he stands in front of me.

I'm standing on a small hill of sand which allows me to be at eye-level with him.

I nod. "I'm baptizing myself."

"Baptizin'?"

"I'm not a perfect person. I'm hoping the water will save me."

"Why do you need savin'?"

I look into his innocent sparkling blue eyes. "I want to be good enough for you."

"You are." His hands find my waist. "You're perfect to me, at least. And that's fine because I ain't perfect either. You already know that."

A smile tugs at my lips. Water rushes against us, forcing us to anchor ourselves by digging our toes into the sand.

"We don't need baptizin'," he says. "I like us the way we are."

Austin's blue eyes burn mine as he holds me tight against him. I feel his body heat through our wet clingy clothes.

"Austin…"

"Yes?" His whisper is barely audible over the howl of the night air and the crashing of the waves.

"Could you really see a life with someone like me?"

"Someone like you?"

"When your mom tells the church you're dating an agnostic woman, what will they say?"

He chuckles. "I don't care what they're gonna say."

129

I pull on my lip. His hands dig harder into my hips. I rest my forehead against his. I can't bring myself to say those words even though I want to… but it doesn't matter. He already knows.

"Don't ever let me go," I say.

"I won't," he says. "I never will."

He kisses me as the salty sea air blows over our cooled skin. The waves rise and the arms of the ocean pull us deeper below the surface. Austin grabs my hand and leads me back to shore. The water doesn't make it easy for us as our feet sink deep into the sand. Austin and I finally emerge, our wet clothes clinging heavily to our skin.

We leave a trail of water and sand as we find our room. Austin turns the water on in the shower before reaching for the clean white towels. When he turns around, he knows that I don't want or need a towel. I drop my wet top to the floor. My pants are next as I step out of them. My skin shivers as my wet hair drips around me. I look unapologetically up into his eyes. My nipples constrict fiercely under the cold drips of water. He drops the towels. His eyes scan my body before returning his gaze to mine. He pulls off his shirt and lets it fall at his feet. The wet shorts come off next and he's just as naked as I am. A small noise escapes my throat as I try to quiet my shaky breath. Austin walks over and stands in front of me, blocking out the light with his broad shoulders. Using his fingertips, he gently grazes the skin on my neck, moving down my shoulder, the curve of my breast, and the small of my waist. I shiver under his touch. He kisses me like I belong to him… because I do.

"I never want you to doubt me, Graceless." His lips whisper against mine.

I look into his eyes. "It scares me how much I like you."

130

He kisses me again. Too turned on to wait any longer, he lifts me and wraps my legs around his waist. He steps into the shower where the steam rises around us. The lemongrass scent of the hotel soap fills the air. The humid air and Austin's warm chest are more than enough to keep away the cold of the ocean. Austin ravishes my neck, kissing my collarbone as he fondles my breast, warming my nipple. He pushes my back up against the cool tile as he presses his body between my legs. He's aroused, touching me, teasing me, toying with the idea of going further.

"Does that feel good?" He asks.

"You always feel good," I breathe.

He pushes against me further, deeper. A moan of surprise escapes my throat, as a needy masculine groan escapes his.

"Deeper," I whisper again.

He holds me tighter, going deeper still until my body is flush with his. He lets out a sigh of relief. I lean my head back against the wall as I hold on tight to him, feeling the sand on his skin. Austin grinds rhythmically, pushing me to a point of insanity. A frenzied desire flashes in his eyes.

"Let's come together." His voice is rough and breathy in my ear.

There's that commanding side of him. I can't hold back when he speaks to me like that. Pleasure threatens to take over. Closing my eyes, I curl my toes and arch my back.

"Yes," he whispers. He grazes his teeth against my neck as we ride the wave of pleasure together. We come together, just like he wanted.

We stand in the hot water for as long as it takes for our legs not to feel like jelly before making our way to the bed. My body is still shaking and pulsing with pleasure. He holds me securely in his arms, sealing me against his body.

As he holds me, I find myself in a euphoric haze. I wonder if I should tell him I love him. They're just three little words. What could go wrong?

Is that meeting halfway?

Unsure what halfway even is anymore, I drift to sleep as the waves crash outside.

— 12 —

GRACE

A few weeks go by as I follow Austin and the team on the road. When I get tired of traveling, I go back to his apartment in Seattle. It's strange living in the apartment without him. Everything in the apartment smells like him—his sheets, the clothes in his closet, the soap in the shower. But without him around, I've become used to calling the apartment my temporary home. He comes back once or twice a week, while I follow him once or twice a week. It's the perfect blend of Austin time and me time.

I've also been spending enough time in Seattle to become a regular volunteer at different shelters and churches nearby. I've been helping the local nuns with their program to feed the hungry. I helped them create an inventory of all the donated goods. Donations always pile up around the holidays and this Thanksgiving is no different.

One day while Austin is still making his way back from Cleveland, I help the nuns clean up after a free chili lunch for the hungry. We're in the kitchen in the basement of the

133

church. I'm pouring the chili into empty containers for anyone who might show up later.

"Do you always have this much food leftover?" I ask as I fill the tenth container.

"It's almost Thanksgiving, so we get a lot of extra food to cook this time of the year," Sister Mary says. Two nuns work at this church—Sister Mary and Sister Ethel. Sister Mary is the bubbly one.

Sister Ethel looks at the containers piling up. "A few people will come by tonight or tomorrow. Sister Mary and I will likely share a portion. But we won't get through these. Especially not on a Wednesday."

"What's special about a Wednesday?"

"The men's shelter down the street gives out hot chicken sandwiches."

Sister Mary stares wistfully at the pot which is still a quarter full. "All that food… it's a shame we can't give it all away!"

"There are worse problems than having too much food," Sister Ethel says.

"Why don't I take a few portions to the women's shelter?" I ask. "The shelter doesn't have hot food like this. They're probably eating bread and cold cuts right now. Do you mind if I bring them a portion or two? There are only three women there right now, and one of them has a child."

The nuns look at each other and nod.

"If there are three women and a child, bring four. And a fifth for yourself!" Sister Ethel says.

"Oh, wow! That's too kind but I don't need any food. I already have dinner plans."

"Nonsense! You need to eat just like everyone else." She pushes five containers over to me as Sister Mary hands me a bag.

"Thank you," I say. "I truly appreciate this."

"We appreciate you, Grace," Sister Mary says. There's kindness in her eyes. "You truly live up to your name."

I smile. "I spent lots of time in and out of shelters and churches when I was young. You two deserve all the praise."

Sister Ethel eyeballs me. "Have you thought about becoming a nun?"

I laugh. "I can't say that I have."

"She can't be a nun," Sister Mary says.

"Why not?"

"Look at her face—she's smiling! There's a man in her life."

"Please tell me it's God," Sister Ethel says.

"Not the way she's smiling." Sister Mary smiles coyly.

I laugh. "I'm not smiling *that* much."

I lower my head as I focus on putting the containers of chili in the bag.

Sister Ethel lets out a sigh as she makes her way to the exit. "I have to go do my prayers. Sister Mary, with all those accusations—you should too!"

Sister Mary smiles at me. "Shall we see you on Thursday?"

"I won't be back until next week. It's a busy schedule…"

"Yours or his?" She asks.

I smile at her. "Goodbye, Sister Mary."

Heading out, I drop the chili off at the women's shelter before heading to the mall. I look around a bit before checking the time and making my way to the fountain.

"It's about time!" A familiar female voice says. That southern twang is undeniable.

"Crystal!" I rush over to her. "It's so weird seeing you in Seattle."

She smiles and poses. "Does Seattle suit me?"

135

She's wearing a loud jumpsuit and a jean jacket.

I laugh. "Very much so."

Crystal throws her arms around me. Her perfume smells like Barbie hair. "I missed you!"

"I missed you too. I'm so glad you were able to come visit!"

"Yeah, well… I'll never say no to a free trip." She squeezes me. "Isn't this great? You're so much closer now! I can actually come out and see you!"

"It's true… my heart feels lighter seeing you."

"And where's your cell phone? You never answer my texts."

"I don't have one yet."

"Girl, you're nuttier than a squirrel in winter. Come on, let's get you a phone." She marches me over to the cell phone store.

We look around at the different models as she shares all the gossip from Tennessee. I have no interest in the personal lives of people I haven't spoken to since high school but Crystal clearly enjoys talking about them, so I let her speak.

"Anyway, after Joey and Isabel made out, I knew it was confirmed."

"Who?" I ask.

"Oh, never mind." She cocks her head slightly. "How about you? You've been *real* quiet about Austin. One day you were trying to avoid him at his birthday party, next thing I know you're in Seattle with him."

I smile. "Yeah… it's been crazy. Things are… good."

"It must be if you're still out here." She smiles happily. "I'm so excited! You two are *perfect* for each other. He's like the butter to your bread."

I laugh. "Can't I be the butter?"

"Oh, Austin is *definitely* the butter, hon. Have you ever seen him walk from behind?"

"Mmhmm, I definitely have."

A young male attendant with a barely-there mustache pops up and joins us. "Can I help you?"

"Yeah, my friend here is a crazy person and doesn't own a cell phone... can we find one for her?"

"Absolutely!" He says with forced enthusiasm.

"Good, because there are aliens in space who are easier to contact than her."

The attendant looks at me. "What are you interested in? Storage space? Battery life? Display resolution? Camera specs?"

"Err... I don't know what half that stuff means." I look at Crystal.

"If you get a good camera, you can send me selfies of you and Austin," she says.

"Selfies?"

I'm not a selfie person. It's easier to be mysterious when my image isn't floating around on the internet. The thought of taking selfies with Austin and sending them to Crystal makes my heart pound. Is that our next step? Would that make us official? Austin has already called me his girlfriend... what's next?

After coming to terms with my very real feelings for Austin, my head is spinning. If we go even a little bit beyond what we've been doing, then we're officially going past halfway. I think I'm ready, but my body shivers with anxiety when I think about it.

"Grace—" Crystal pulls me from my thoughts. "Just pick a phone... do it for me. You don't have to text anyone but me... please."

137

Relaxing my shoulders, I nod. With the attendant's help, I pick out a phone that's small and uneventful. I only need it for texting Crystal, and maybe texting Austin. I might also take a personal photo or two of him—nothing risqué, just something for my eyes only when he's not around.

With my shopping bag in hand, I walk with Crystal through the mall. We have a reservation for dinner in ten minutes.

"So..." I clear my throat. "About me and Austin... you still haven't told my brother, have you?"

"Joe? No... I don't see him too often. He's a real travelin' businessman."

Exhaling, I relax my shoulders. "Good. It's better that he doesn't know."

"Why?"

I shake my head. "Telling him would be so... official."

"And official is bad?"

"Well, not bad... just... official."

"Hey!" Austin's voice rings out.

I freeze. "Austin? What the... what are you doing here?"

He's standing in front of the restaurant waiting for us.

"I texted him," Crystal says. "When he sent me the plane ticket, I told him our plans. I didn't want to come all the way out here without seeing him!"

"I was able to move my schedule around and come back earlier." Austin brushes his shoulder against mine. "I hope I'm not intrudin' on girl time."

Eyes still wide from the surprise of seeing him, I shake my head. "Not at all."

"Crystal—you look great, as usual."

"Oh, thanks." Crystal does her little pose again before hugging Austin. When they're done, Austin shifts his focus

138

to me. It's been a few days since I've seen him and I can tell we've both missed each other.

"Hey." He smiles a soft but sexy smile.

"Hey," I say softly.

With no shame, he steps forward and kisses me. The cowboy scent that he leaves around the apartment doesn't compare to the real thing. His real scent reminds me just how intoxicating he is in real life.

"Aww!" Crystal coos.

Pulling away from Austin, I wipe my lips and look shyly over at Crystal. She's smiling with glee. I can see the excitement in her eyes.

"Umm... excuse me," she says. "You two are cuter than a June bug!"

I get the sense that she'll be telling someone back in Tennessee about this before the end of dinner.

"Thanks." Austin chuckles. "Grace definitely makes me feel cuter."

I shake my head at him. "Don't encourage her."

"Are you kidding?" Crystal puts her arms around us. "I love this. Come on, let's get dinner."

After being seated and ordering our food, we drink and share stories about Tennessee and high school. Conversation flows and laughter comes easily between us. It makes me think that I made a mistake leaving for so long when we could have been hanging out all this time.

"Aww, I love you two as a couple!" Crystal says as she finishes the last of her pina colada. We're a few drinks in.

A couple? My belly stirs. I'm not sure if it's from the strawberry daiquiris or something else.

"Can I take a picture of you two?" Crystal clutches her phone.

Austin puts his arm around me.

"I don't think so," I say.

"No!" Crystal protests. "Why not?"

"I don't like having my picture taken," I say. "Besides... my mouth is all red from the daiquiris."

"Fine." Crystal disappointedly puts her phone back on the table and sips on the last bit of her drink. "You know what? We should do this again. The Blades are playing in Tennessee soon, aren't they?"

"That's right," Austin says.

"Just in time for Thanksgiving! I can organize a turkey dinner, stuffing, the works."

Austin looks at me. "What do you think?"

"I..." I swallow past the lump in my throat. Going back to Tennessee as a couple is a big commitment. We'll have to tell Austin's parents. We'll have to tell Joe. Being put on the spot, I go with the easy answer. "Sure."

"Great!" Crystal claps her hands excitedly. "This calls for more drinks. Waiter!"

***

Later that night, we drop Crystal off at her hotel before going back to our apartment. Things between us are more quiet than usual as we get ready for bed. It's the first time since he's been back from a road trip that we don't immediately rip off each other's clothes.

"Hey," Austin says. He's standing over the sink brushing his teeth. "Are you sure you want to go back to Tennessee?"

"Sure... why not?"

"I know you, Grace Lawless. I can tell when you're uncomfortable."

I shift from one foot to the other.

"You're uncomfortable right now," he says.

I look into his blue eyes. "I'm fine with going. It's just... if we go back, then that means this is real."

Putting his toothbrush down, he takes my hands in his. "It already is real."

"Then we'll have to tell Joe."

He looks into my eyes as if studying my expression. "You don't want to tell him?"

My throat feels dry. I don't say anything. My eyes tell him everything he needs to know.

"I see." His shoulders drop slightly. "If you don't want to, then we can't wait."

"Oh... okay."

His head drops. "Alright."

Avoiding my gaze, he looks away. It makes me wonder if he wanted me to say something different. He doesn't want to meet halfway anymore. He wants to go all the way. He wants to tell everyone, including Joe. He pulls back but I tighten my grip on his hands.

"Hey..." I tug on his shirt so that he'll face me again. "Halfway, right?"

He pauses and looks around—everywhere but me. "I've gotta go to bed."

Without any further discussion, he pulls away. Feeling like I've done something wrong, I follow him to the chilly bed.

141

— 13 —

AUSTIN

After tossin' and turnin' all night, I get up early. Grace is still sleeping. We only get to share the bed a few times a week. I'm tempted to roll over and spoon her but I can still feel last night's tension. I saw the uneasiness in her eyes when I unexpectedly showed up to dinner. And she got real quiet when Crystal called us a couple. She spent most of the time after that pushin' food around her plate.

She still doesn't want to commit to anything. We won't be able to tell Joe about us. I've been keeping this secret from him for way too long. It doesn't feel right holdin' it in much longer.

Quietly getting out of bed, I make my way to the kitchen and make coffee. I fill a pan with bacon and put it on the stove. I get lost in my thoughts as I mindlessly stare at the pan while the bacon sizzles.

"Hey," a quiet voice says. Grace is standing behind me in her silky white sleep shorts and oversized Blades t-shirt. Her dark hair is long, tousled, and wild.

142

"Hey," I say. "Sleep okay?"

"Not really." Her big hazel eyes watch me.

"Thinkin' about last night?"

She nods. "I don't want to drive a wedge between us… but I want to stay where we are for a bit."

"And where are we?" I ask. "Because you didn't look too happy about hangin' out with Crystal last night. Hell, I was surprised she even knew about us!"

"Of course, she knows about us!" She clutches her stomach. "Why are you using that tone?"

"Because I'm annoyed! I've been telling you all this time how much I want you, how I'll lay my life down for you."

"And I've been telling you I only wanna meet halfway. Are you the only one who gets what he wants?"

"No." I sigh. "But where the hell does that leave us? Relationship purgatory?"

The corner of her mouth lifts slightly.

"I can't help myself," I say. "I'm passionate… and I'm passionate about you." My skin is getting hot. Composing myself, I look away and flip the bacon. The grease pops and sizzles.

"All I know is that I really like you," she says. "Like a lot."

I shake my head. "It's hard believin' that when you got so uncomfortable around the idea of us bein' a couple."

"I just… I need time to think about it."

Closing my eyes, I pinch the bridge of my nose. "Do you even like livin' here?"

Her mouth falls open. "Of course, I do!"

"Because you never leave your stuff here. I'll find a toothbrush and empty bags of potato chips—that's it. Your bag is always packed up and ready to go."

"Because we travel together, don't we?" She says defensively. "Isn't that why you invited me out here? To travel with you?"

"Well, yeah..."

"What do you want me to do? Buy junk and leave it everywhere?"

"No. I just want to know that you're not gonna disappear again."

The room goes quiet. She looks away.

"You're a man of faith," she says. "Can't you have faith that I'll stay?"

I exhale. "You once told me faith's not enough."

She doesn't respond.

"Grace, I'm not tryin' to be a controlling prick," I say. "I'm not tryin' to keep tabs on you or anythin'. I know you're a bird and you're gonna fly—that's what you do. I just need a sign that you're stickin' around."

Her chin quivers as she looks down and away. My heart breaks seeing her so vulnerable like this. But it's hard not to take any of this personally. I know it's not personal. She has her own reasons for being reluctant about committing to relationships. But after almost three months together, I thought our connection would rise above that by now.

"I know you want a life with me," I say in a low voice. She looks up at me. "I can see it in your eyes. You just won't allow yourself to believe it."

Her lips part but she doesn't say anything. The alarm on my phone goes off.

"I've gotta shower and get ready for practice." I pull the bacon off the burner and shut off the heat. "Leave some bacon for me."

Without saying anything else, I head to the bathroom and take a shower.

There's only so much I can do. I promised to meet her halfway and that's where we met. I don't want to be doomed to a lifetime of spending holidays at home alone, lying to my best friend. I know I told her she could have one foot outside the relationship, ready to leave if she wanted. But I expected that foot to get chilly eventually and step inside.

Steam fills the room as the hot water rushes over my shoulders. I close my eyes and drop my head back. A soft voice says something behind me. Turning around, I see Grace in the shower with me. She's naked, wild, and beautiful. Her wild dark hair hanging over her breasts makes her look like a mysterious mermaid. White clouds of steam rise around her.

Pulling my head down, she presses her nose against mine. "I do want you," she says.

Touching her waist, I pull her warm body against mine. Her skin feels impossibly soft and perfect.

"I don't want to mess this up," she whispers.

"Me neither."

"I want to go to Tennessee with you," she says. "We'll figure it out from there."

A slow smile spreads over my lips and I nod. "Okay."

Pressing my lips against hers, I kiss her as if I've never kissed her before. The water rushes over us. When I break the kiss, she lets out a tiny whimper of protest.

I press my nose against hers again. "We made it through our first fight."

She smiles. "Was that really a fight?"

"I don't like sleeping that far away from you." I hold her tighter against me. As she runs her hand down my back, I feel myself rise to attention.

"Make it up to me, then," she says. That sexy smile of hers gets me every time.

I nod. "Yes, ma'am."

***

The team is in the New Orleans airport waiting for a flight to Tennessee. We're playing against the Memphis Rockers tomorrow. It gives me enough time to see Grace, Joe, and the whole family.

I'm sittin' with the guys at our gate. They're making fun of Jack Lalonde for his long hair. A ten-second video of Jack and his luscious hair at last night's New Orleans game went viral.

"You broke the internet!" Logan says. "Dude!"

"Look at that hair," Cooper says. "It's almost as nice as mine."

"Do you use conditioner?" Ricky asks. "Or is that from all the essential oils your girlfriend uses?"

The guys laugh.

"Come on! Tell us your secrets, Flow!"

"Flow? Seriously?" Jack shakes his head as he tucks his hair under a black Blades hat. "You guys laugh... but I think the hair makes me more aerodynamic."

"Welcome to my world!" Cooper says. He's leaning back, hands behind his head. "I've been saying that for years."

Shaking my head and smirking at their antics, I check my phone. Even though Grace has a phone now, she sure doesn't use it. Getting ahold of her is harder than doing advanced algebra. But I'm a patient man. I know I'll see her tonight.

When we arrive in Memphis, it's the early afternoon. Making the twenty-minute drive out to Woodstock, I visit my parents first, gettin' all the latest news about the farm. After doin' all my son duties—mainly fixin' the Wi-Fi and eatin' Ma's turkey gravy sandwiches—I head out in the direction of the Lawless house. The sky is already a shade of dark purple. Grace should be there by now. And so should Joe.

When I arrive at the Lawless house, I notice that Joe's truck is absent from the driveway. Pulling up, I notice lights on inside. Movement too. Shutting off the engine, I climb out of the car and make my way up the familiar yellow door. I knock before pushing my way inside. I've been here hundreds of times. I'm no stranger to walking in unannounced.

"Hello?" I call out. I don't hear anything.

Making my way through to the kitchen, I find Grace searching through the fridge. She's wearing headphones and she's humming along to the music.

I smirk. "Why do I always find you in the kitchen?"

Pulling the headphones out of her ears, she turns her head slightly so that I can see her profile. "You're early."

"Am I?" I walk over and slip my arms around her from behind. "I thought I was perfectly on time."

"Are you alone?" She strains to look around.

"Mmhmm." My lips find her neck as I inhale the scent of jasmine and vanilla that lingers on her skin.

Her body curves perfectly against mine as I hold her against me.

"You must have really missed me," she says.

"Is it that obvious?" I smirk as my lips graze her neck.

As she leans her head back on my shoulder, her hair cascades down my arm, tickling the surface of my skin. My

147

fingers slip under her waistband, finding the impossibly soft skin underneath.

"I've been dreamin' about touching you," I whisper.

She reaches back and tangles her fingers in my hair. "Keep talking."

"I've been dreamin' about peelin' off your clothes, holdin' you on my lap, and usin' my hands to explore the sensitive skin of your inner thighs—"

"You've been dreaming of tickling me?"

"Not tickling you… making you squirm and moan a little bit."

I feel the heat flaring under her skin as I press my lips against her neck. Turning around, she lifts onto her toes as she presses her nose against mine.

"I missed you too," she whispers. She kisses me. Her seductive lips are impossibly soft. And she tastes just as good as she smells.

The front door clicks open and Grace instantly pulls away from me. She fixes her shirt and makes sure her hair isn't out of place. I have a feeling that means she's not ready to tell Joe about our relationship status yet.

"Howdy." Joe walks into the kitchen with a case of beer balanced on his shoulder. "I came prepared!"

"Oh no, you've still got that mustache?" I look at the caterpillar on his top lip.

"What, you don't like it?" He looks at Grace. "What d'ya think?"

She shrugs. "I guess it's a slight improvement to that face of yours."

He shakes his head. "Sheesh! What a warm welcome from my dear little sister."

"Don't ask for an opinion if you can't handle it," she says.

I chuckle.

Joe looks at both of us. "So y'all been catchin' up?"

Grace and I look at each other. What the hell am I supposed to say?

"Yep," Grace says. "It's been so long since we've seen each other… it's hard to even know what to catch up on."

She says it with such confidence that even I believe her. She looks over at me for a split second and I can tell she's apologetic. I can tell she wants to talk about this.

Joe walks over to the fridge. "You know what we need? Some fried chicken to go with this cold beer."

He slides the case of beer into the fridge before pulling his keys out of his pocket.

"Let's go pick some up." He looks at me. "We'll bring it back and eat here."

I don't want to pick up chicken. All I wanna do is talk to Grace. I want to figure out if there's a way out of this mess.

"You comin', Grace?" I ask.

She shakes her head. "I'll wait for you guys here."

"Suit yourself," Joe says. "Come on, Austin. I've got bones to pick about yesterday's game in New Orleans. By the way, did you see Jack Lalonde's flow? Hey, why aren't you coming?" He stops at the front door.

"Go ahead," I tell him. "Let me just umm… let me just grab my phone."

"Alright. Giddy up, cowboy! Don't leave me waitin'." Joe leaves. The front door squeaks before shutting behind him.

I look at Grace. "What does Joe know about us?"

"Nothing."

"Is that what you want him to know?"

Her big hazel eyes look at me. She hesitates. "If I say yes, will you be mad?"

149

I sigh. "I just… I don't wanna lie to Joe."

"You're not lying."

"Well, I ain't tellin' the truth."

She shakes her head. "It's just weird being back in this house again with Joe, and you… I just need time."

Time.

"You still don't want anyone to know we're together?"

She sighs in frustration. "Austin, please don't do this right now."

"When, then? How much longer am I supposed to keep this secret from my best friend?"

"Why do you keep rushing me?"

A pang of guilt twitches in my stomach. "It's true, I've been pressuring you. But only because I wanna be with you so bad, Graceless. And when you're not leavin' any possessions in our apartment, and you're pretendin' you don't have a life with me… it starts to feel personal."

She swallows. "I… I see. But I can't rush my feelings to accommodate yours."

I look into her eyes. "Alright, then."

The truck's horn honks outside. I can feel the tension and the heavy breathing between me and Grace.

"Joe's waitin'," I say. "Will you stick around to have dinner with us?"

"Yes," she says softly.

"Good." I back away. "Do you want crispy chicken or regular?"

"Crispy, obviously."

"That's my girl."

She finally smiles. Turning, I make my way out through the squeaky yellow door before climbing into Joe's big truck.

150

Closing my eyes, I rest my head back against the seat and exhale.

"Trouble finding your phone?" Joe starts the engine.

"Yeah… I misplace it sometimes." My mind is still spinning.

Joe pulls the truck out of the driveway and takes off down the road. "It's good having you back, man."

"Yeah… it's good bein' back. How've you been?" I try to refocus my attention on Joe.

He shrugs. "Can't complain. I own the most popular car wash in Tennessee and the second most popular car wash in Arkansas and Mississippi."

"Just second, huh?"

He laughs. "Don't bust my balls… I've only got a few locations out there right now. I'm still buildin' my empire."

A country song on the radio fills the gaps in conversation.

"Crazy that you and Grace are here on the same weekend," Joe says.

"Yeah, well… it's Thanksgivin' weekend."

That answer seems vague enough to avoid suspicion.

"I guess she's finally spending holidays here again." Joe takes a right turn onto the main road.

"That's somethin' to be thankful for." Tapping my foot, I check my phone.

Joe reaches over and squeezes my shoulder. "You okay, man? You're tenser than usual."

"Am I?"

"Is it trouble on the ice? I can give you some pointers, you know…"

I chuckle. "It ain't anything like that."

"Then what is it?"

Looking out the window, I stay silent.

151

"Come on, man. You can tell me," he says.

I exhale. "It's girl trouble."

Joe laughs in shock. "You? Girl trouble? I guess I should have expected it... Mary-Beth still talks about being heartbroken by you."

"You gossip about me with her?"

"Not really. I went on a date with her a few months back. She talked about you the whole time. Serves me right for breaking the bro code. I hope that's okay, brother."

"Don't worry about it," I say. "We're beyond the bro code."

I hope.

"Heh, yeah." Joe pulls into the drive-through of Poco Pollo—the fried chicken restaurant. He orders more food than three people could possibly eat before we're instructed to wait. He puts his arm up on the headrest and turns to face me. "So, tell me about your girl troubles."

I shake my head. "It's complicated... every time I take a step closer, she takes a step back."

He chuckles. "What are you two doing? Dancin' or something?"

Smirking, I shake my head. "I want something serious with her."

"Wow. She must be pretty special."

"Yeah, I mean... she's perfect. I'd marry her right now if I could."

"*Perfect?* Wow, she must be pretty special." Joe furrows his brow. "Why haven't I heard of her until now?"

I shake my head. "She doesn't want anything serious. I can't force anythin'."

Joe sighs. "That's rough, man. I don't know what to say. If I'm being completely honest, I don't have the best advice

152

when it comes to women. I still haven't quite figured 'em out yet."

"Yeah... me neither, apparently."

The drive-through attendant leans out the window and hands Joe two big bags of take-out. Joe hands them to me as the scent of fresh fries and fried chicken fills the car. I take a deep euphoric inhale.

"Damn, I missed this chicken." The scent of it makes me forget about my relationship situation for two seconds.

"Come on, let's get home and crush this. The beer's waitin'."

As we drive back, I think about how to handle dinner with the Lawless siblings without giving anything away. I'm realizing that I did this to myself. Grace told me from the very beginning that nothing would be official between us. She told me upfront what she wanted, so I can't be mad. But dang, I'm a competitive guy and it sucks to lose.

— 14 —

GRACE

Sitting in the dark, I look up at the dimly-glowing stars on my bedroom ceiling. The front door squeaks open downstairs. The guys are back. I can hear them chatting downstairs. I feel like I'm back in high school. I'd always be trying to focus on homework but Austin's voice was too distracting. He always managed to lure me downstairs.

Gnawing on my lower lip, I debate whether I should go down and join them. I told Austin I would, but hiding away would send him a message—that I'm protesting his pushiness. Every time I give him an inch, he takes a mile. He wants me to come to Tennessee and announce our relationship to Joe, his parents, and who else? He has to know that he can't dictate everything anymore.

I hear them laughing loudly downstairs. As I stare at the slowly fading stars on the ceiling, I decide not to hide anymore. I'm not sixteen anymore, I'm a grown woman. If I want Austin to know how I'm feeling, I'll put my feelings right in front of him.

Getting off the bed, I avoid the creaky floorboards as I make my way downstairs. The scent of fried chicken welcomes me as I walk into the dining room. Austin's blue eyes instantly connect with mine.

"Gracie!" Joe points at the chicken with his greasy hands. "Better get in here quick. We're inhaling this stuff."

I take a seat across from Joe and next to Austin.

"I thought you left," Austin says.

"I said I'd join you guys, didn't I?" I happily fill my plate with a few pieces of fried chicken and some coleslaw.

"This is just like old times!" Joe says. "Didn't think I'd ever be sitting here with you two again."

Austin and I exchange a look.

Joe laughs as he licks his fingers. "Who woulda thought that Austin and I would be rich, while Grace—the one with the highest marks in school—would be the unemployed and broke."

"Hey," Austin says defensively.

"It's fine," I say. "At least I don't have to look in the mirror and see that mustache."

Joe laughs. "Jealous… all of you."

He takes another bite of chicken.

"Life's not about money anyway," I say.

"Bullshit," Joe says. "Life's easier with money."

"What's it about, then?" Austin looks into my eyes.

Good question.

"Helping others," I say. "That's why I volunteer with the nuns."

"Still broke though," Joe says.

"Is that life for you? Money?"

"Nah, partying and having fun. But money helps a lot with that." He pulls a full tub of coleslaw over and starts eating straight from the container.

"And you, Austin?" I look at him.

"I like all the things money can't buy—skills, gym gains, family, intimate relationships…"

Joe looks up from his coleslaw. "My boy's gone all soft ever since he got a girlfriend."

I look up with a sharp gaze. "What? *Girlfriend?*"

With a hard stare, Austin keeps his steady gaze on me.

"Maybe you can give him advice with his girl problems."

I raise my brow. "You've got girl problems?"

Austin shakes his head. "It's nothing. I have no girl problems."

"That's not what you told me," Joe says. "She doesn't want anything serious but Austin does. He was trying to find a way to fix that."

"*Fix* that?" I look at Austin. "She's not ready for something serious, so there must be something wrong with her?"

He shakes his head. "Nothin' needs fixin'. I just gotta accept it, that's all."

"Nah, that's not what you said," Joe says. "You said you wanted to marry her."

"Joe, will you shut the hell up for once?"

I exhale sharply. "Can't you just be happy where you are? Why does anyone want anything serious anyway?"

"Why *wouldn't* someone want somethin' serious? Love, friendship, family…"

"Do you love her?" Joe asks.

Austin and I both look at him. It feels like the air has been sucked out of the room.

156

"What?" Austin asks.

"Do you love her?" He repeats. "I'm just trying to figure out how serious this really is."

Realizing that my mouth has fallen slightly open, I close it. I look over at Austin, curious about his answer. His blue eyes stare deep into mine.

"I love her more than anythin'," he says. His gaze doesn't waver.

There's a beat of silence as I stare at him. "Say that again."

He clears his throat. "I love her more than anythin' in this damn world."

The world falls away as I stare at him. Thoughts pop in and out of my head before I realize how much time is ticking by. I don't know how to react. I don't know what to say.

Joe takes a break from devouring a full container of coleslaw to stare at us. "What the fuck is going on between you two?"

I keep my eyes on Austin. I feel like I can see his thoughts. Something on the table lights up—it's Joe's phone.

"It's the Memphis location," he says, reading the screen. He answers the call. *"Hello? Oh, hey Earl!"*

Austin is still staring at me with that hardened stare.

"Oh, really? Yeah, I think I've got the files on my laptop. Let me just go find them—no, no, it's alright. It won't take long." Joe gets up and leaves the room, leaving me and Austin alone.

"You're talking to Joe about us?" I break the silence first.

"He asked about my life. I told him I was datin' someone. I didn't tell him it was you."

"Clearly."

"Grace—I have to talk about my life with my best friend. You're part of my life now, Grace. I love you." He exhales. "It feels good to finally say that. I love you. *I love you.*"

157

I close my eyes and touch my temples. "This is *just* what you do… you tell me you're not pushing me, and then you tell me you love me!"

"I ain't pushing you."

"Bullshit! You're like a hyperactive golden retriever puppy swinging your tail and knocking everything over."

"Puppies are cute, though. Right?"

I suppress a smile as I shake my head. "Don't be cute with me right now."

Austin drags his chair closer and leans forward. His delicious masculine scent displaces the scent of fried chicken and beer.

"What?" I ask.

"Don't you have something to say to me?"

"I thought you weren't pushing me."

"I know you love me." His gaze is heavy on me. "I see it in your eyes."

I stare at the masculine features of his face for a few seconds before shaking my head and looking back down at my plate. "If you see it, then why do you need me to say it?"

He leans in. "Because I want to hear you say it."

I put down my fork. "Do you really want me to say I love you for the first time over greasy fried chicken?"

"You could tell me you love me over a pile of garbage. As long as you tell me you love me, I don't care what's happenin' around us."

Exhaling forcefully, I face him. "Why do you always get everything you want?"

He touches my knee. "Not everythin'."

The conversation between us goes silent. Joe is still talking loudly on the phone in the other room.

Austin drops his voice a bit deeper. "What are you afraid of, Graceless?"

I poke the food around my plate. "What happens when you get bored of me?"

He laughs. "Grace, I know you. You can't scare me away. I'm in this for the long haul."

Silence fills the air as I collect my thoughts. I take a deep breath and look into his eyes. "I don't know if I can be responsible for making you happy, Austin. I can barely keep myself happy."

He furrows his brow. "Don't I make you happy?"

"I don't want to rely on a man for happiness."

"You ain't relyin' on me," he says. "It's a team effort."

There's a strange comfort in knowing I'm not alone. His hand is still on my knee.

"Grace... don't you love me?" He raises his eyebrows hopefully. "Have these last few months meant nothing to you?"

"Austin—"

A floorboard creaks and Joe enters the room. "Damn, that was a long call."

Austin pulls away from me.

Joe sits back at the table. "Instead of buying ten units, the manager at the Memphis location ordered ten *cases* of hot pink rubber mats. I know people love pink, but I'm not sure they love it *that* much."

He rubs his hands as he surveys what's left of the chicken.

"Good. You left some for me."

If there's any tension lingering between me and Austin, Joe clearly hasn't noticed it. He continues eating.

"I'm not hungry anymore," I say. Rising from the table, I grab my plate.

159

Austin gets to his feet.

"It's fine," I say, waving him down. "You can hang out with Joe."

"You don't want to spend time with us?" He asks.

I shake my head. "I need some time alone."

He watches me for a moment.

"It's alright," Joe says. "She can entertain herself."

Austin doesn't move as he watches me leave.

"I hope you took all the chicken you want," Joe calls out. "Because we're finishing off the rest!"

Ignoring him, I put my plate in the sink and head upstairs. Sitting in my dark room, I stare up at the faint glow-in-the-dark stars on the ceiling.

I want to tell him I love him because I do. But if I'm in love, why does it feel so scary?

**

Never getting a chance to talk to Austin before bed, I wake up feeling lost. I'm assuming he's sleeping in the basement, or at his parents' house. We ended things on such strange terms last night that I don't know how to feel today. Pulling on a pair of stretchy black pants and an oversized wool sweater, I head downstairs. It's a chilly but sunny November day. Sunshine is streaming through the house. Joe is already in the kitchen eating out of a bag of beef jerky.

"Breakfast of champions, I see." I pour myself a glass of water before downing it in one go.

"It's just an appetizer before I eat last night's leftover chicken."

"There were leftovers? I thought you said you guys would finish it off."

160

"Nah… Austin was in a weird mood last night."

"Ah…" I don't ask him to elaborate.

"You got plans today?" He asks.

"Yeah… I'm going to Crystal's place for lunch."

"Fun, fun." He stuffs another piece of beef jerky into his mouth. "Hey, before I forget—do you have any interest in selling the house? I'd need your signature if you do."

I pause. "You're selling the house?"

He nods. "It's about time, isn't it? Mom's room has been empty for years now and so has yours. Besides, I'm rarely around. I'm always on the road visiting the Sparkle and Shine locations anyway."

"Where will you live?"

"I'll find a smaller place, something more modern—a condo or something."

"You won't miss that big backyard?"

"Maybe I'll get a condo with a backyard," he says.

Chuckling, I look around at the old kitchen. I've had so many memories here—memories with Mom, memories with Austin. My throat tightens at the thought of giving up those memories.

"It'll be sad to let this place go," I say.

"You can keep it if you want, but I figured since you're never here, you'd be okay with splittin' the profits."

"Well… it *is* kind of nice knowing I can come back to my old room whenever I want…"

"Yeah, at least you'd have a real home and you won't be drifting around the world like a hobo."

"A real home," I mumble.

I think about the apartment in Seattle. It's truly starting to feel like my home. I like waking up and sharing a coffee with Austin in the morning. I like looking out at the bay when the sun is setting. I like snuggling in my favorite spot on the couch. And I love falling asleep in Austin's arms in that big bed of his. *Of ours.* How nice it would be to finally just accept it.

"If I get a condo, I'd make sure to get one with a guest bedroom for you if you visit," Joe says. "And Austin too… but if you're ever over at the same time, you'll have to fight over who gets the room and who gets the couch."

I laugh. "I think I can win him over."

Reminded of last night's friction with him, my smile fades quickly. It's enough for Joe to notice.

He furrows his brow. "You alright?"

I look at him. "I have to tell you something, Joe."

"Do you want money again?"

"No, nothing like that…" I swallow. "I've been feeling conflicted… about my boyfriend."

He raises his brows. "Your boyfriend? When did this happen?"

"A few months ago… at Austin's birthday party actually."

"You're dating a Tennessee boy?" He asks. "Oh god, it's not one of the Boyens brothers, is it? I *knew* I shouldn't have invited them!"

"No," I say. "It's Austin."

My heart is racing in my chest. I expect Joe to get angry or annoyed. Instead, he laughs.

"That's hilarious," he says. He looks around. "Is he here? Is he filming this?"

"It's not a prank." My voice shakes. "And I think I fucked things up because we had a fight and… well, you heard him yesterday."

Joe looks like he's in complete disbelief. "Wait a minute… you're telling the truth?"

162

I nod.

He absently chews on another piece of beef jerky as he stares off into nothingness. "Why didn't he tell me?"

"He wanted to tell you, but I told him not to... telling you just felt so *real*. And now it's actually real..." My face flares with heat.

There's no going back now.

"So, *you're* the girl who won't commit to him?"

"Yes."

"And he *loves* you."

My throat feels dry. "I guess he does."

"Wow." He chews on another piece of beef jerky as he stares into the distance again. "I can't believe this."

"I know... it's weird for me too. But I really like him."

"So? Why are you two fighting?"

"I don't know... after seeing what happened between Mom and Dad, I just assumed happy endings didn't exist."

"*Pfft,* Dad was a dick," he says. "Austin is *not* like that. And if he ever does what Dad did, I'll kick his ass."

"Ha! I'd like to see you try and kick his ass."

"Oh, I can take him!" Joe stands taller, showing off his scrawny frame and that ugly mustache. "I've taken him on before!"

I laugh. "Maybe when you were thirteen."

Joe deflates a bit. "I swear I can still take him."

Crossing my arms, I lean back against the counter. "Why do you and Austin always think I need some sort of protector?"

"We don't think you *need* one. But you're our family. If we can't make sure you're okay, what are we good for?"

I smirk. "So, you're not mad about me and Austin?"

163

"I mean, I'll definitely kick his ass later… but I'm happy for you guys. At least I know you're with someone I can trust and *not* a Boyens brother."

Chuckling, I grab a piece of beef jerky and start chewing. A weight has been lifted off my shoulders. I'm annoyed I didn't do this sooner.

"Lots of memories here," I say, looking around the kitchen.

"Yeah… good ones. Friends and family."

"Friends and family," I repeat under my breath.

I think about which category Austin is in, and which one I want him to be in.

"It'll be weird not being able to come back to this place," I say. "After all our moving around, this is the place we've lived in the longest."

"Yeah, but sometimes moving on is the best thing to do. That's how you evolve."

Narrowing my gaze, I watch him for a moment. He still has the same smiling eyes he had when he was a boy. "When did you get so wise? Is it the facial hair?"

"Being a prodigy entrepreneur helps." His mustache barely conceals his self-confident grin.

"I don't think your ego needs any praise, but I'm proud of you."

His expression softens. "Thanks, sis. You should visit more often. I miss ya."

"I miss you too." I smile. "Just FYI… if you get a condo with a hot tub and a full guest bathroom, I'll be visiting a lot more often."

"Full guest bathroom? Weren't you staying in hostels, using outhouses and shit? When did you get so bougie?"

I laugh. "Austin's been a bad influence on me."

164

"I'm gonna figure out how to make you *both* sleep on the couch."

"Good luck with that." I grab the leftover chicken out of the fridge. "Should I heat some for you?"

He checks his watch. "Actually, I've gotta get ready. I'm driving to Memphis to watch the Blades game. Wanna come?"

"Oh... I wish I could, but I promised Crystal I'd see her."

"Ah, well. Maybe next time." He spots the bucket of leftovers in my hands. "Eat as much chicken as you want... I can always get more."

He pulls away.

"Joe?"

He stops. "Yeah?"

"Don't hurt Austin too bad. He wanted to tell you all along. It was me who wasn't sure."

He nods. "Thanks for telling me."

Once the yellow door squeaks and Joe is gone, I reflect on our conversation. I'm glad I told Joe. It was the right thing to do. And maybe if I let go of the past, I can finally evolve too.

— 15 —

AUSTIN

That morning, I get up early to take a helicopter ride around the farm with Pa. After all the routine checks are done, we have a big breakfast.

"I'm so excited to go to the big game today!" Ma is wearing a blue Blades t-shirt as she scrapes fried eggs out of a pan and onto her plate. The game is against the Memphis Rockers at noon. I'll have a few more hours in Tennessee before heading back to Seattle tonight.

Pa is sipping his coffee and reading the newspaper. He must be the only person in the world who still reads a real newspaper.

"You've been fightin' more than scorin'," Pa says. "Are you gonna fight again today? Or are we gonna see some points from you."

"I don't know." I push the bacon around on my plate.

"I thought you said you were ready to upgrade your skills! Remember? On your birthday?"

"Oh, Norm… stop antagonizin' him," Ma says.

"I just wanna know—where's that drive gone?"

I exhale as I push my plate away. "It's still there."

Ma eyes my plate. "Are you not hungry?"

I shake my head. "I'm tired."

"What, you didn't sleep well last night? I made sure the noise machine was on in your bedroom!"

"It's not that."

She narrows her eyes. "Or maybe you had too many beers with Joe."

Sighing, I rub my face. "Not that either."

I feel exhausted from constantly worrying about Grace. Hell, I don't even know if we're still together… or if we ever were. What are we, anyway? No belongings at the apartment, no 'I love you's'. This relationship is startin' to feel like a kick in the balls.

"Finish your food," Pa says. "You need strength if you're gonna get some points today."

He pushes the plate back in front of me.

Shaking Grace from my thoughts, I nod. "Yes, sir."

A few hours later, I'm on the ice ready to play against the Memphis Rockers. The stands are full and music pumps through the arena. My shoulders are tenser than usual. I stand at the blue line as I wait for the play to start. Exhaling, I look out at the crowd. My parents are here somewhere and so is Joe. I doubt Grace is here—not after last night. Pushing her out of my mind, I try to focus on the game. Pa was right earlier—I haven't been focusing on hockey enough. I've been too distracted this season.

As the game starts, I try to target the left winger on the other team. His name's Gunthry—number fifty-five. He's a scrawny guy, only about six-foot tall, but he's got a heck of

167

an aim. As I block Gunthry's view of the net, Memphis' largest defenseman, Duncan Borse, pushes me out of the way. I lose my balance and slam into the boards. *Ouch.* That's gonna leave a mark. I don't think twice before I'm up on my feet and following the play to the other side of the ice. Logan's got the puck and he's making his way to the opposing net. My eyes are on Borse. He's built bigger than Joe's red truck. I can tell he wants to push Logan off the puck but I'm not gonna let that happen. Adrenaline is flowing through my veins today. Borse picked the wrong day to mess with me. As he reaches for Logan, I push him off course.

"What the fuck? *Ref?*" He looks around for a referee. They're not stopping the play.

"Hey, I'm just doing what you did to me," I say.

"You wanna go? Huh?" He bares his teeth at me—at least, what's left of them.

The play is picking up and moving to the other end of the rink. Even though Borse is the perfect opportunity to release all my frustration, I know I should avoid unnecessary confrontation. It takes everything in me to ignore him. Turning away, I skate down the ice to be part of the play.

"Hey!" Borse chirps. "You too much of a chicken to fight me?"

He laughs obnoxiously. I ignore him.

"Maybe I should make out with your girlfriend," he calls out. "Maybe you'll pay attention to me then."

My ears pound as I grip my stick tighter. My lip twitches into a snarl and all I want to do is drop my gloves. I know I'll get a penalty if I fight him. It wouldn't be good for the team. *The team.* That's all I should care about. Following the play to the other side of the ice, I stay open for Logan. He passes the puck across to me. My way to the goal is blocked but Logan is wide open. I send the puck back to him for an easy goal, but Borse comes out of nowhere and pushes the puck off his stick. The play is heading back in the opposite direction.

I'm really starting to hate this guy.

Picking up my feet, I chase after Borse. As he reaches the blue line, he intentionally slows down. I reach my stick forward in an attempt to poke it off his stick. Borse lifts a skate and stomps down on the blade of my stick. My stick cracks and he goes flying onto the ice in the most blatant dive I've ever seen. I laugh at how obvious it is. Out of the corner of my eye, I see the ref raise his arm and whistle down a penalty. *Good.* Borse deserves it. It's karma for actin' like a buffoon.

"Number eleven for tripping," the referee says.

"Me?" I skate over to him. "But he stepped on my stick!"

The referee ain't listenin'. He's pointing at the penalty box, waiting for me to follow orders like a good little soldier. I look over at Borse who's staring at me with a shit-eating grin. Shaking my head, I grab a new stick before skating across and stepping into the penalty box. I throw my stick against the bench.

This is bullshit.

Faces are staring at me from behind the glass—they're all wearing Memphis jerseys. One guy in particular—a bearded man—is grinning at me as he sips his beer. I ignore him and everyone else as I take my spot in the detention chair.

The game starts up again with the Blades a man short. I'm trying to keep a positive mental attitude, but it's fucking hard when nothing goes my way. How can I be grateful for anything in these conditions?

"*Hey Aaaustin,*" a voice taunts behind me. It's the bearded man with the beer in his hand who's sitting behind the glass. "*Do you miss your girlfriend?*"

Great. I'm gonna have a Memphis fan taunting me for the next two minutes. Tuning him out, I watch as the guys kill off the penalty by keeping the puck out of their zone.

"*Hey Aaaustin, have you been drinking too many soy lattes out in Seattle? You're getting soft!*"

I try to ignore him and watch the play, but he's loud and obnoxious.

"*Or maybe you're eatin' soybeans off your dad's farm!*"

I roll my eyes. If there wasn't a partition between us, he'd be eating those words. It's not like a partition has ever stopped me before.

"*Hey Aaaustin, I know a ten-year-old girl scout who'll fight Borse for you if you're too scared!*"

Grabbing my water bottle, I tilt my head back and squirt a healthy dose into the back of my throat. When I'm done, I aim the bottle higher and squirt water over the glass. I can hear the fans behind me squealing in shock. I smirk to myself as I keep my eyes on the ice. The guys push the puck out of the zone. There are only a few seconds left in the penalty. Getting ready to get back out there, I watch the seconds tick down before stepping out onto the ice. Logan passes me the puck. I've got a chance for a breakaway. I start skating, pushing the puck along. Everyone is far behind me. It's just me and the Memphis goalie. Keeping my eyes on him, I shoot the puck. He bats it away but it comes right back to me. He's laser-focused on me. He's in the zone, but so am I. Out of my peripheral, I see Logan arrive on the other side. I fake the shot before passing to Logan. The goalie takes the bait, diving to the wrong side of the net as Logan easily taps it in.

170

Goal!

Logan and I hug and tap each other's helmets.

"*That's* what I'm talking about!" He says.

"Damn right, brother." I smile.

We do our victory lap, high-fiving the rest of the team before sitting on the bench to watch the replay. The goal—and my assist—are beautiful. And to top it all off, the rest of the game is scoreless, making our goal the game-winner. Staring at the penalty box across the ice, I laugh to myself and shake my head in disbelief. Grabbing a marker from the coaching assistant, I write something on the blade of my stick.

With the stick in hand, I step onto the ice and skate across the rink to the penalty box area. The crowd there is already on their feet and getting ready to leave but they gather at the glass when they notice me approaching. I see the bearded heckler from earlier. He ignores me as everyone else gathers, putting out their hands and hoping they'll get the stick.

"Hey!" I call out, getting the bearded man's attention. He touches his chest in confusion. "Yeah, you. This is for you."

He seems confused at first until I start guiding the stick over the glass to him. He grabs it and I skate away before he has a chance to react or say anything. As I reach the bench, I look across the rink to see him smiling as he reads the message.

"What did you write?" Dean's standing behind me.

"Thanks for the motivation," I say. "With my name and jersey number."

Dean chuckles. "You think he'll be a Blades fan after this?"

I smirk. "Probably not, but at least he might ease up on me next time."

Smirking to myself, I follow Dean down the tunnel and toward the locker room. I really needed that win. I feel like a confident man again. I've got my optimism back.

***

After the game, I get a ride with Joe as he drives back to Woodstock. It's only four-thirty but the sun's already dipping below the horizon. My flight back to Seattle leaves in a few hours.

"That game was sick!" Joe says. "That penalty you got? Fuckin' *stupid*."

"Yeah… but at least it set me up for that assist." Sitting in the passenger seat, I finish whatever's left in my water bottle. "Feels good having numbers next to my name again."

"Always the optimist."

"PMA, right? Positive mental attitude."

Joe's mustache twitches as he smirks. "That's right, brother."

He turns up the country music on the radio. A guy is crooning about spilled beer and a missing dog.

Staring at the road ahead, I sigh. "Joe, I gotta confess somethin'…"

He turns down the radio. "Yeah?"

"Remember how I said I was datin' someone?"

He nods. "I remember."

"Well… here it goes. It's Grace."

I wait for the bomb to go off. I'm only realizin' now that I probably shouldn't have told him while he's driving.

He clears his throat. "I know."

He says it so casually that it takes a second to process.

172

"Uh…" I have too many questions to ask at once. "What? How?"

"Grace told me this morning."

My eyes widen. "She did?"

Grace told him?

"That's right," he says. "She called you her boyfriend."

My chest expands. *She did?* I'm so shocked that I don't know how to respond.

I look over at him. "You're not mad?"

"Oh, I am. I'm still gonna fight you after I park the car." He looks over at me and laughs.

I reluctantly laugh with him. "Don't fuck with me, Joe…"

He shrugs a shoulder as he steers down the highway. "I mean… I *did* wanna wring your neck at first. It's a shocker, for sure. I mean, you and Grace… who woulda thunk, right? And why wouldn't you guys tell me?"

"Yeah." I rub the back of my head. My hair is still damp from the post-game shower. "I should have told you sooner."

"Well… Grace told me not to blame you. Now that I know you're dating Grace, the commitment issues you were talking about yesterday make sense."

"Heh. Yeah."

"I know she can be flighty, always traveling… like a bird. But you two make sense together."

I raise my brows. "You do?"

"Yeah… the free-spirited traveler and the good ol' southern boy. The bird and the bear. It's weird but it works. And maybe you'll get her to come out to Tennessee more often. Hell, you already have!"

I exhale as lightness takes over my body. "I'm glad you approve of us."

173

"Of course, man. I know you'll treat my sister with respect. You have to, or else I'm gonna come for you."

I chuckle. "I'll never hurt her."

"Good, because I've never seen my sister emotional over someone like this before."

"Emotional?"

He nods. "Her voice was all shaky and her eyes looked all sad… I know Grace pretty well. I can tell you guys had a fight or were taking a break or somethin'."

That flood of relief I just had quickly gets displaced by anxiety. "Is that what she called it? A break?"

"Not exactly," he says. "She said she fucked things up between you two. I didn't ask for the details, but she was clearly upset."

"I see." I stare at the road ahead as Joe pulls onto their street and parks in their driveway.

Getting out of the car, I push through the squeaky yellow door. The house is dark.

"Grace?" I call out. There's no response.

I climb the stairs. Her bedroom door is open.

"Grace?" I scan the room. Her overnight bag is nowhere to be seen and the bed is made.

Where is she? I pull out my phone and check the transactions on our shared credit card. She hasn't used it. And I haven't sent her a plane ticket to go back to Seattle yet… would she even want to go back home? Does she even consider it home? I have too many questions and no answers.

"Joe?" I call out.

"Yeah?" Joe's in the kitchen scrolling through the Chinese take-out menu on his tablet.

"Do you know where Grace is?"

174

He looks up from the screen. "She was supposed to hang out with Crystal today."

"Umm, okay... I'm gonna borrow your truck." I grab his keys off the counter without even waiting for approval from him. "I've gotta look for Grace."

Joe shrugs nonchalantly before looking back at the tablet. "Do you want egg rolls?"

"No, thanks." I'm already halfway out the door.

Within ten minutes, I'm pulling up outside Crystal's house. Seeing that it's dark inside, I drive another few blocks to her mom's house. Cars are parked up and down the street. I'm assuming their big family is at their house for Thanksgiving dinner. I walk up and ring the doorbell. There's so much commotion inside that I have to ring it twice. After a few seconds, Crystal answers the door. Her face lights up at the sight of me.

"Austin! Are you here for the party?" Music is streaming out of the warm room behind her. I can hear people laughing and talking inside. "I didn't realize that my mom invited you!"

"She didn't." I try peeking into the busy house. "I'm here for Grace. Is she here?"

Crystal sympathetically raises her brows and tilts her head. "Oh, honey... I drove her to the airport a few hours ago."

"The airport?"

She nods.

"Well... where'd she go? I didn't send her any plane tickets."

Crystal shakes her head. "I don't know... she seemed distracted. She said she'd figure out where she was going once she was at the airport. Are you guys still together?"

I shake my head. "I don't know."

175

Sighing, I run my hand through my hair. It finally happened. She's gone. Unreachable.

"I'm sorry," she says. "I begged her to stay but we both know how elusive Grace can be. She's like smoke… you can see her and feel her presence, but the moment you try to grab her, she's gone—like a ghost."

"Hmm." I process her words.

The sound of laughter filters out from inside.

"Are you sure you don't wanna come in for some turkey dinner?" She asks.

I shake my head. "No, thanks. I gotta go."

"Don't be a stranger, now!"

Pulling away, I get back into the big red truck. I don't agree with what Crystal said. Grace ain't a ghost. She's real, and I won't let her disappear again. Pulling out my phone, I dial her number. The call goes straight to voicemail. I close my eyes and pinch the bridge of my nose.

"Hey, Grace," I say in a stern voice. "This isn't how I wanted to do this but I don't know where you are and I can't reach you. I fucked up. I'm man enough to admit it. I shouldn't have pushed you. You told me what you wanted from the beginning and I ignored you. I disrespected you by pushin' you." Sitting alone in the truck, I look down and shake my head. "You deserve more than that. I wanna do better. I wanna be better for you. I know you're out doing your own thing, and I respect that… but I want you in my life. I *need* you in my life, Graceless. If you want to travel the world, we can do that together. I'll quit the team, I swear I will. And if you want to travel alone, that's cool too. I'll even meet you halfway if you want… and I mean that literally. We can meet in France for French toast or in Prague for pretzels… I don't even know where the hell Prague is or if they even have pretzels there, but maybe we can find out

176

together." I sigh heavily. "I'm goin' on a tangent… I'm just callin' because I'm sorry. I did the one thing I didn't wanna do—I pushed you away. I don't know what's in the future for us, Grace… but I know I want you to be a part of mine."

I run my hand through my hair and look around. People are coming out of the house to smoke. The noise from the party spills out onto the street.

I turn away to get a sense of privacy. "This call is getting long… if this is the last thing you hear from me, I just want to say that I love y—"

The voicemail beeps and cuts me off, leaving me stunned for a moment. Tossing my phone onto the passenger seat, I lean forward and press my head against the steering wheel. It feels cool against my burning forehead. I don't even know if Grace has her phone or if she left it behind before going to Timbuktu—or wherever she might be off to. I let out a heavy exhale. Sitting back up, I put the car in drive and head back to Joe's place.

***

It's almost midnight when I arrive back in Seattle. It's raining and it's cold enough that the raindrops are turnin' into snowflakes on their way down. As a big guy who gives off a lot of heat, I try to be grateful for the cold weather. Instead, all it does is make me miss Tennessee. It also makes me dread facing my empty apartment. With Grace there, it was finally startin' to feel like home. Now that's gone and it's just an empty shell. And even worse—there'll be signs of her. My bedsheets will still smell like her, and I'll still see strands of her dark hair around the apartment. I guess I was wrong when I said she never left anything behind.

177

Feelin' remorseful and ashamed of myself, I feel like I deserve to be punished. I'm gonna be sittin' on the couch tonight, eating a turkey sandwich alone on Thanksgiving.

By the time I get into my building, I'm drippin' wet. The rain soaks through my jacket and I'm shivering. After getting off the elevator, I shake my wet hair and push my way into the apartment. The lights automatically turn on when I step inside. It's even emptier and quieter than I expected. I drop my stuff by the door and look around. No empty potato chip bags on the kitchen counter, no ballet flats by the door. Walking across the room, I sit on the couch and drop my head back. I let out a heavy sigh.

Maybe we're just not meant to be together.

As I stare up at the ceiling, the lights go out. I'm left blinking as my eyes adjust to the light. Furrowing my brow, I notice glowing stars on the ceiling.

"What the—" I sit up and look around. The ceiling is covered in them.

"Do you like it?" A feminine voice asks.

I look around and see Grace standing behind me. The light from the hallway outlines her silhouette from behind. Her long dark hair hangs on either side of her soft face. She looks angelic in the dim light.

"Grace…" I get up and slowly walk over to her. "When did you get here?"

"A few hours ago. I wanted to come back and add a little bit of myself to the apartment." She points up at the glowing stars.

I'm still staring at her in shock. "I thought things were over between us."

"I… I was afraid they were too," she says softly. Those big hazel eyes look up at me. "I hope they're not."

178

I take a step closer. "I've always got faith in us, Grace. PMA, right?"

A smile appears on her lips. "PMA."

My heart is pounding in my chest.

"I'm ready to evolve," she says. "I still love traveling, but I can't bear the thought of leaving you... you're my home, Austin Berr."

Warmth floods through my chest.

"Can I live here with you?" She asks. "Will you tolerate my chip crumbs in your apartment?"

I laugh.

"Of course." I touch my chest. "I've never had a Thanksgiving where I felt this thankful before."

Her beauty radiates as she smiles.

"And I won't need you paying for everything anymore," she says. "Joe and I are selling the house in Tennessee. I'll be getting a share of the money, so you can keep the credit card you gave me."

I want to tell her to keep the credit card but I know she'll resist. I have more money than I can even dream about spending in one lifetime. Besides, nothing I want in life can be bought. Not even millions in the bank can buy this moment.

"Money is useless to me," I say. "All I want is you."

I stare at the woman I know I'm gonna marry. It might not be soon, or even until we're old and gray. But I know I'll marry her one day if she'll let me. And I'll do my best to convince her to let me. With the way she's looking at me right now, I don't think it'll be very hard.

Unable to resist, I pull her closer. "I missed you."

"I missed you too." She smells like lemongrass soap and dill pickle chips. "And I love you."

179

My neck prickles with heat. I finally get to hear her say those words.

"I love you too."

Her neck moves as she swallows. "I'm ready to go all the way."

I smile as I push a dark strand of hair off her cheek. "One step at a time. Come here."

Cradling her head, I press my lips against hers. Suddenly all the pieces of my life seem to fit together. I understand what I have to look forward to. I know what I'm working for, and what I'm fightin' for. And even though this is just the beginning, we're way past halfway. We're going all the way, and nobody can stop us.

– EPILOGUE –

GRACE

The spring flowers are already starting to bloom around the Tennessee house. The front lawn is covered in prairie buttercups and Virginia bluebells.

When I told Austin about the plan to sell the house, he insisted that we buy it. The decision was a no-brainer. The house is sentimental to us—it's where we first met, where we first kissed, and where I found out that Austin loved me. It means we'll have our own place to stay whenever we come back to visit. And Austin's excited about the big backyard and the extra land—he calls it his retirement plan. I'm pretty sure he just wants to have a reason to fly around in a helicopter every morning like his dad does.

Sure, I want to evolve—but after years of running away, coming back home *is* evolving. And we've been slowly transforming the place into our dream home by renovating everything inside.

Up on the living room wall are pictures of Joe, my mom, and Austin. Austin's parents are up on the wall too. The kitchen is completely renovated to include the kitchen island and extra fridge space that I've become accustomed to in Austin's apartment. The marble countertop and the white tile backsplash complement the freshly painted peach walls. Everything is so beautiful that I feel a spark of joy. It's a far cry from my hostel days. Despite knowing I have my own bank account, Austin still spoils me. Not that I'm complaining. After all, he helped me buy and renovate this place. It still has the squeaky yellow front door and the beautiful backyard view, but it's now designed to fit us. It's home.

Making my way upstairs, I go to our new room. We left my old room untouched but combined the other two rooms into one. The master bedroom is now spacious enough for Austin and me, including a bathroom and a walk-in closet. The closet is mostly for Austin's many jerseys, suits, and shoes, but I'm slowly building up a wardrobe that's more than just a few tank tops and elephant pants. I actually have a presence now. I have a space, and I have a community— neighbors, friends. I'm not just a ghost drifting around the world. Even though I still have the traveling bug.

Pulling out my travel bag, I place it on the bed and start filling it with clean clothes. I make sure to pack my deodorant and hairbrush too. Zipping it up, I place it on the ground before checking the time. It's late. Almost ten o'clock. I check my messages from Austin. The last time he messaged me was over twelve hours ago. He was finishing up some loose ends in Seattle today, but his flight should have landed over an hour ago. *Where is he?*

Feeling nervous that he's not home yet, I text him and ask where he is. I feel silly. I like to think I'm carefree and coolly detached. But at a moment like this, I realize just how hopelessly obsessed with him I am. I shouldn't be impatient.

After all, I've got all summer to spend with him. The Blades had their last game of the season last night and it only took an hour after the loss for Austin to book us tickets for a summer trip to Europe. He said he didn't want to waste a single second together. It'll be the first time we get to spend time together without hockey interrupting us every other day.

I check the time again. Clutching my phone, I head downstairs and look out the front window. The street is just as dark and quiet as it usually is. Unsure what to do, I go back to the bedroom. Pulling on my silk shorts and cotton tank top, I climb into bed and get under the covers. It's hard to ignore my phone but I need to sleep to prepare for the long flight tomorrow. Austin is probably just delayed.

Restless, I toss and turn a few times before drifting off to sleep. I feel myself shiver in the cold breeze before a fire shines brightly around me, keeping me warm. I feel the warmth on my face, like sunshine kissing me. The flames of the fire close in around me, enveloping me in warmth. Breathing in, I smell the scent of embers and cedarwood mixed with distressed leather. I feel Austin's lips on my neck. He's spooning me as his large hands press tight against my body.

My eyes flutter open. It's not a dream. His body is perfectly curved against mine. He pushes the strap off my shoulder before tracing his lips over my sensitive skin.

"Is it you?" I blink into the light. "Or am I dreaming?"

He gently laughs. "Close your eyes. Go back to sleep."

"Where were you?"

"It's a long story… there was a minor car accident. Everything's fine. But my phone didn't survive and I ended up missin' my flight."

"Oh my god!" I try to sit up but he holds me in place.

183

"I'm fine." He pushes my hair off my neck and continues kissing me. "I'm here now. And we've got forty minutes until we gotta leave."

I relax back into the bed. "Forty minutes?"

"Mmhmm." He breathes me in. "I just wanna stay here for a bit."

His hand moves lightly down my belly and traces over my thighs. Eventually, he finds his way between my legs. His fingers tease me so slowly that it borders on torture. I press my head back against his shoulder and moan.

"We get to go on vacation together," I whisper.

"Mmhmm." His neck vibrates against mine. "That's right. All that travellin', yet there's only one place I want to be."

His fingers explore a bit deeper and my breath hitches. Austin's watching me, making sure he's doing the right things. He definitely is.

"We'll be in Amsterdam in twenty hours," I say, struggling to speak between moans. "Nothing says we have to leave the hotel room."

He chuckles. "That's true... hey, how are you still speakin'? Maybe I've lost my touch."

"You haven't," I breathe.

He wiggles his fingers, hitting all my favorite spots. I finally lose my ability to speak as I drop my head back against his shoulder. His magic touch makes forty minutes disappear pretty quickly. When I finally beg him to stop, he holds me in his arms and kisses me. Inhaling his delicious scent, I realize I'm truly in cowboy heaven.

I smile. "Imagine if I never kissed you all those years ago on the basement couch?"

"You still woulda kissed me at Applelooza."

184

"Maybe…"

He smirks. "Doesn't matter. I woulda made sure we ended up together."

"Are you sure? Because I had to make the first move twice."

He chuckles. "Is that how you want this to go?"

His hand grazes over my belly, tickling me. I push him back and he holds me close. I kiss him.

"We're gonna miss our flight," I say.

"I already missed one… at least this time, it'll be worth it." He kisses me again.

We don't get to hear the yellow front door squeak that day, or the next either. Europe can wait… I waited six years for Austin, and he was worth every second.

Thank you for supporting indie authors!

If you liked this story, please leave a review and let me know so I can write more like it!

-Violette

Want more? Keep reading...

Rule Breaker

(A Jacksonville Stallions Book)

Hockey phenom Brendan Baker's messy breakup is starting to manifest in poor gameplay on the ice—and the hecklers in the crowd aren't going easy on him. When the team owner invites Brendan to stay at her house as he gets back on his feet, he realizes that the ruthless heckler from the previous game is the owner's daughter. Now Brendan has to make a good impression on both of them to secure his future with the team.

If you love a spicy forced proximity hockey romance, then grab "Rule Breaker " and start reading!

Also by Violette Paradis

Bad Boys of Hockey

The Seattle Blades are sexy, rebellious, and always ready to heat up the ice!

Logan - *A Fake Boyfriend Hockey Romance*

Jack - *An Opposites-Attract Hockey Romance*

Rory - *A Second Chance Hockey Romance*

Cooper - *An Opposites Attract Hockey Romance*

Verona - *A Secret Baby Hockey Romance*

Dean - *Boss-Employee Hockey Romance*

Austin - *A Second Chance Brother's Best Friend Hockey Romance*

JACKSONVILLE STALLIONS

Always up for a challenge, the Jacksonville Stallions are hungry to prove themselves.

Rule Breaker – *An Enemies-to-Lovers Hockey Romance*

Icy Temptation – *A Grumpy/Sunshine Single Dad Fake Fiancé Hockey Romance*

Offside Attraction – *A Secret Identity Enemies-to-Lovers Hockey Romance*

Visit www.violetteparadis.com for more

188

Milton Keynes UK
Ingram Content Group UK Ltd.
UKHW010119011223
433552UK00004B/215